R. K. ISSACS THOMAS

The Book Of Ethan

Three Stories of Deception and Redemption

First published by Workhorse215 Publishing 2026

First edition

ISBN: 979-8-234-06058-7

This book was professionally typeset on Reedsy.
Find out more at reedsy.com

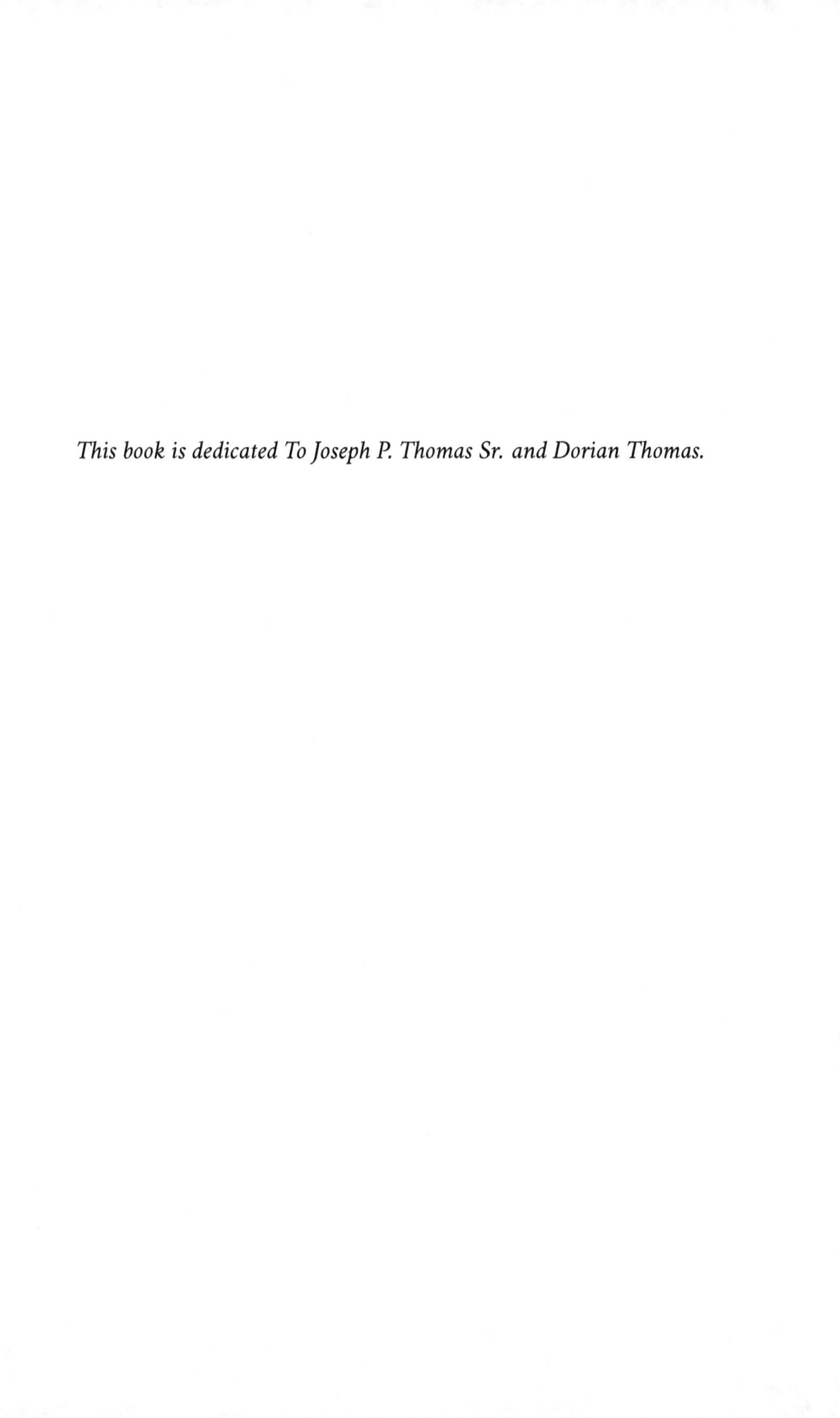

This book is dedicated To Joseph P. Thomas Sr. and Dorian Thomas.

Contents

I

The Book of Ethan

Written By R.K. Issacs Thomas Sr.

One

Chapter 1

The Spark of Ambition

In the heart of the bustling city, where dreams are made and crushed with equal fervor, there lived a man named Ethan. Once a charismatic salesman, he danced on the edges of success, enticed by the allure of wealth. Yet, his ambitions led him down a treacherous path, where the boundaries between right and wrong blurred, and morality became a distant memory.

He began with nothing—no silver spoon, only a burning desire to escape the bottom. Ethan quickly learned that people don't buy products; they buy possibility. That insight became his gospel.

From hawking low-end goods, he ascended to brokering fine art, gold, and the world's rarest diamonds. His charm opened doors; his hunger closed deals. And soon, the name Ethan Thorne became synonymous with persuasion itself.

In his relentless pursuit of success, he gradually lost sight of its true meaning. He quickly amassed immense wealth, mastering the psychology of persuasion, but losing his guiding principles in the process. Ethan's silver tongue charmed his clients, his promises of fortune captivating their imaginations. With each sale, his pockets grew heavier, his ego inflated. But behind the façade of prosperity lay a darker truth—a man consumed by greed, willing to bend the rules to satisfy his insatiable desires.

Two

Chapter 2

The Master's Edge

At the height of his power, Ethan thrived in a world where truth and illusion were indistinguishable. Ethan operated in a thrilling, dangerous space where truth was only as valuable as its perceived worth. He knew the difference between a salesman and a con artist was a fragile thread: a salesman delivered what was promised and a con artist didn't.

Yet, in the world of seven-figure paintings and undocumented gold, those lines often blurred. Ethan didn't lie about provenance—he simply crafted irresistible narratives, expertly omitting inconvenient truths that disrupted the buyer's fantasy and left out the parts that might dull the dream.

A flaw in a diamond? He called it character. A questionable painting? A rediscovered masterpiece. He once convinced a European baron that a flaw in a massive diamond wasn't a defect, but a signature imperfection, proof of its authenticity and uniqueness. He built castles of desire in his clients' minds—always leaving one haunting question: Did they truly know what they bought, or only what Ethan wanted them to believe?

Ethan built entire worlds in the minds of his clients—palaces of promise. But when the applause faded and the rooms grew silent, his reflection became harder to face. His wealth swelled, but the silence in his penthouse grew heavier, thick with unspoken guilt.

He had mastered the sale but lost his soul in the transaction.

Three

Chapter 3

The Unseen Thread

While Ethan's empire shimmered, far below the surface, a quiet man began to pull a single thread. Unbeknownst to Ethan, his arrogance had finally drawn the eye of an unlikely adversary.

Officer Leo Vance, a rookie detective in the Economic Crimes Unit, wasn't dazzled by luxury or titles. This rookie stumbled upon an inconsistency in the shipping manifest of pre-Columbian gold artifacts.

The dialect in the dated customs document didn't match the regional language of that period—a minute detail, invisible to most, but glaring to obsessively meticulous Vance.

That single inconsistency became Vance's mission. And without knowing it, Ethan had just been marked. Vance wasn't after headlines or promotions; he was after precision. And now, quietly, meticulously, he was after Ethan

Thorne.

Four

Chapter 4

The Chill of Surveillance

The downfall began without warning. The first signs weren't loud or noticeable. No sirens. No warrants. It began with a nervous art handler refusing to share documents. Then a liaison abruptly quit, citing "new compliance concerns." Ethan's once-fluid network grew silent. Ethan's gut tightened with a dread he hadn't felt in years. His contacts confirmed it: Officer Leo Vance was asking questions—quietly, surgically and not about flashy diamonds, but about forgotten legal footnotes buried in his gold trades.

Ethan, the master reader of desire, realized he was now being read himself. The thrill of the chase had inverted. The hunter had become the quarry. The thrill of control was replaced by the cold awareness of a trap closing in.

Five

Chapter 5

The Jewel and the Noose

Desperate for one last, flawless move, Ethan turned to The Falcon's Eye—a twelve-carat, deep sapphire-blue diamond, rumored to have been cut from a meteorite of legendary origin. It was so rare that it was too valuable to be tainted.

The jewel's story was so mythic it was nearly unsellable. Ethan crafted a pitch rooted not in greed, but in truth—selling it to an eccentric billionaire as a symbol of legacy and philanthropy. As the buyer's hand extended to seal the deal, salvation seemed within reach until the door burst open.

"Ethan Thorne," came the voice of Officer Leo Vance. "You're under arrest for fraud, money laundering, and illegal handling of artifacts. The game is over." The handshake froze midair. The honest sale was complete—but the reckoning had arrived.

Six

Chapter 6

The Final Confinement

The trial was a media spectacle — Ethan's final stage. Cameras flashed, headlines screamed, and Ethan turned the courtroom into a theater of charm. No words could outshine the meticulous evidence compiled by Vance. He tried to sell his innocence with all the charm and charisma that had once sold fortunes, but the evidence spoke louder than his silver tongue.

Convicted on all counts, Ethan was sentenced to twelve years in a maximum-security facility. Yet, even there, he didn't break. Within six months, he adapted—turning prison into his newest market. His gift for reading people made him indispensable. He became the Consigliere of Commerce, orchestrating contraband flows, mediating disputes, favors, and controlling the underworld economy from behind bars. Ethan Thorne had lost his freedom but found his next empire. He found his element. The prison became his new marketplace.

Seven

Chapter 7

The Blood Bond and the Betrayal

Ethan's underground empire thrived—until his ambition once again crossed a fatal line.

He brokered an illicit "body sale," arranging a secret medical operation for a powerful inmate. The plan imploded in betrayal, and Ethan was left bleeding from a near-fatal stab wound.

As he lay bleeding in the infirmary, doctors discovered his blood type was very rare. It required an immediate, compatible donor. Only one local match existed and that was none other than Officer Leo Vance. The transfusion saved Ethan's life. And when he learned that this blood type was shared only among immediate family, realization struck like lightning: the man who had caged him was his brother. Ethan's world shifted. His relentless pursuer wasn't just his nemesis.

Eight

Chapter 8

The Ultimate Trade

Lying weak but alive, Ethan did not dwell in emotion—he calculated how he could capitalize from this event.He requested a private meeting with Vance. When they met, the air between them was thick with unfinished history.Ethan revealed the truth of their bloodline and offered his final, audacious deal.In exchange for Vance using his influence to secure Ethan's early release, Ethan would give him the one thing he could never find through law enforcement—the truth about their family's past and their fractured lineage, a secret Ethan had uncovered years earlier.It wasn't blackmail. It wasn't mercy. It was a business negotiation. The master salesman was selling his own redemption to the one man who embodied justice. And Vance was left with an impossible choice between his duty to uphold the law or honoring the blood they shared.

Nine

Chapter 9

The Book Closes

No one knows what decision was made in that silent, guarded meeting.Some say Ethan Thorne was quietly released months later under mysterious circumstances. Others claim Vance refused the offer, leaving his brother to die behind bars.But one truth endures: Ethan Thorne sold everything there was to sell—truth, loyalty, and even blood.And in the end, what he bought was immortality in the shadows of his own legend.

The End

II

En Espanol

Ten

Capitulo 1

La chispa de la ambición

En el corazón de la bulliciosa ciudad, donde los sueños se forjan y aplastan con igual fervor, vivía un hombre llamado Ethan. Antes un carismático vendedor, bailaba al borde del éxito, atraído por el atractivo de la riqueza. Sin embargo, sus ambiciones le llevaron por un camino traicionero, donde los límites entre el bien y el mal se difuminaron y la moralidad se convirtió en un recuerdo lejano.

Empezó sin nada—sin cuchara de plata, solo un ardiente deseo de escapar del fondo. Ethan aprendió rápidamente que la gente no compra productos; compran posibilidades. Esa visión se convirtió en su evangelio.

De vender productos de baja gama, ascendió a la intermediación de arte fino, oro y los diamantes más raros del mundo. Su encanto abrió puertas; su hambre cerró tratos. Y pronto, el nombre Ethan Thorne se convirtió en sinónimo de persuasión misma.

En su incansable búsqueda del éxito, fue perdiendo poco a poco de vista su verdadero significado. Rápidamente acumuló una inmensa riqueza, dominando la psicología de la persuasión, pero perdiendo sus principios rectores en el proceso. La lengua de plata de Ethan cautivó a sus clientes, sus promesas de fortuna cautivaron su imaginación. Con cada venta, sus bolsillos se volvían más pesados, su ego inflado. Pero tras la fachada de prosperidad se escondía una verdad más oscura: un hombre consumido por la codicia, dispuesto a doblar las reglas para satisfacer sus insaciables deseos.

Eleven

Capítulo 2

El filo del maestro

En la cima de su poder, Ethan prosperaba en un mundo donde la verdad y la ilusión eran indistinguibles. Ethan operaba en un espacio emocionante y peligroso donde la verdad solo valía tanto como su valor percibido. Sabía que la diferencia entre un vendedor y un estafador era un hilo frágil: un vendedor entregaba lo prometido y un estafador no.

Sin embargo, en el mundo de las pinturas de siete cifras y el oro sin documentar, esas líneas a menudo se difuminaron. Ethan no mentía sobre la procedencia—simplemente creaba narrativas irresistibles, omitiendo con destreza verdades incómodas que rompían la fantasía del comprador y dejaban fuera las partes que podrían apagar el sueño.

¿Un defecto en un diamante? Lo llamó personaje. ¿Un cuadro cuestionable? Una obra maestra redescubierta. Una vez convenció a un barón europeo de que un defecto en un diamante enorme no era un defecto, sino una imperfección de la firma, prueba de su autenticidad y singularidad. Construyó castillos de deseo en la mente de sus clientes—dejando siempre una pregunta inquietante: ¿Sabían realmente lo que compraban, o solo lo que Ethan quería que creyeran?

Ethan construyó mundos enteros en la mente de sus clientes—palacios de promesas. Pero cuando los aplausos se desvanecieron y las habitaciones quedaron en silencio, su reflejo se volvió más difícil de enfrentar. Su riqueza creció, pero el silencio en su ático se volvió más denso, cargado de culpa no expresada.

Había dominado la venta, pero perdió su alma en la transacción.

Twelve

Capítulo 3

El hilo invisible

Mientras el imperio de Ethan brillaba, muy bajo la superficie, un hombre callado empezó a tirar de un hilo. Sin que Ethan lo supiera, su arrogancia finalmente había llamado la atención de un adversario improbable.

El agente Leo Vance, un detective novato de la Unidad de Crímenes Económicos, no estaba deslumbrado por el lujo ni por los títulos. Este novato se topó con una inconsistencia en el manifiesto de envíos de artefactos de oro precolombinos.

El dialecto del documento de aduanas anticuado no coincidía con el idioma regional de esa época—un detalle minucioso, invisible para la mayoría, pero que llamaba la atención del obsesivamente meticuloso Vance.

Esa única inconsistencia se convirtió en la misión de Vance. Y sin saberlo, Ethan acababa de ser marcado. Vance no buscaba titulares ni promociones;

buscaba precisión. Y ahora, en silencio, meticulosamente, iba tras Ethan Thorne.

Thirteen

Capítulo 4

El Frío de la Vigilancia

La caída comenzó sin previo aviso. Las primeras señales no fueron fuertes ni perceptibles. No hubo sirenas. No hubo órdenes judiciales.

Todo empezó con un manipulador de arte nervioso negándose a compartir documentos. Luego un enlace renunció abruptamente, citando "nuevas preocupaciones de cumplimiento." La red antes fluida de Ethan se quedó en silencio. El estómago de Ethan se apretó con un temor que no sentía en años.

Sus contactos lo confirmaban: el agente Leo Vance hacía preguntas—en voz baja, quirúrgica y no sobre diamantes llamativos, sino sobre notas legales olvidadas enterradas en sus operaciones de oro.

Ethan, el maestro lector del deseo, se dio cuenta de que ahora le estaban leyendo a él mismo. La emoción de la persecución se había invertido. El cazador se había convertido en la presa. La emoción del control fue reemplazada por la fría conciencia de una trampa que se acercaba.

Fourteen

Capítulo 5

La joya y la soga

Desesperado por un último movimiento impecable, Ethan se volvió hacia El Ojo del Halcón—un diamante de doce quilates, azul zafiro profundo, que se rumoreaba había sido tallado de un meteorito de origen legendario. Era tan raro que era demasiado valioso para ser contaminado.

La historia de la joya era tan mítica que casi no se podía vender. Ethan elaboró una propuesta basada no en la codicia, sino en la verdad—vendiéndola a un excéntrico multimillonario como símbolo de legado y filantropía.

Cuando la mano del comprador se extendió para cerrar el trato, la salvación parecía al alcance—hasta que la puerta se abrió de golpe.

"Ethan Thorne", dijo la voz del oficial Leo Vance. "Estás arrestado por fraude, blanqueo de dinero y manipulación ilegal de artefactos. El juego ha terminado."

El apretón de manos se congeló en el aire. La venta honesta estaba completa—pero había llegado el ajuste de cuentas.

Fifteen

Capítulo 6

El confinamiento final

El juicio fue un espectáculo mediático — la última etapa de Ethan. Las cámaras destellaron, los titulares gritaron y Ethan convirtió la sala en un teatro de encanto. Ninguna palabra podía eclipsar las meticulosas pruebas recopiladas por Vance. Intentó vender su inocencia con todo el encanto y carisma que antes vendió fortunas, pero las pruebas hablaban más alto que su lengua de plata.

Condenado por todos los cargos, Ethan fue sentenciado a doce años en un centro de máxima seguridad. Sin embargo, ni siquiera allí se rompió. En seis meses, se adaptó—convirtiendo la prisión en su nuevo mercado. Su don para leer a la gente le hacía indispensable.

Se convirtió en el Consigliere de Comercio, orquestando flujos de contrabando, mediando disputas, favores y controlando la economía del hampa desde la cárcel. Ethan Thorne había perdido su libertad pero encontró su siguiente imperio. Encontró su elemento. La prisión se convirtió en su nuevo mercado.

Sixteen

Capítulo 7

El vínculo de sangre y la traición

El imperio subterráneo de Ethan prosperó—hasta que su ambición volvió a cruzar una línea fatal.

Negoció una "venta de cuerpos" ilícita, organizando una operación médica secreta para un interno poderoso. El plan se vino abajo en traición y Ethan quedó sangrando por una herida de arma blanca casi mortal.

Mientras yacía sangrando en la enfermería, los médicos descubrieron que su grupo sanguíneo era muy raro. Requería un donante inmediato y compatible. Solo existía una coincidencia local y no era otra que el oficial Leo Vance.

La transfusión salvó la vida de Ethan. Y cuando supo que ese tipo de sangre solo se compartía entre la familia inmediata, la realización lo golpeó como un rayo: el hombre que lo había encerrado era su hermano. El mundo de Ethan cambió. Su perseguidor incansable no era solo su némesis.

Seventeen

Capítulo 8

El Oficio Supremo

Tendido débil pero vivo, Ethan no se detuvo en las emociones—calculó cómo podría sacar provecho de este acontecimiento.

Pidió una reunión privada con Vance. Cuando se encontraron, el aire entre ellos estaba cargado de historia inconclusa.

Ethan reveló la verdad sobre su linaje y ofreció su último y audaz trato.

A cambio de que Vance usara su influencia para asegurar la liberación anticipada de Ethan, Ethan le daría lo único que nunca podría encontrar a través de la ley: la verdad sobre el pasado de su familia y su linaje fracturado, un secreto que Ethan había descubierto años atrás. No era chantaje. No era misericordia. Era una negociación de negocios.

El maestro vendedor vendía su propia redención al único hombre que encarnaba la justicia. Y Vance se quedó con una elección imposible entre su deber de hacer cumplir la ley o honrar la sangre que compartían.

Eighteen

Capítulo 9

El libro se cierra

Nadie sabe qué decisión se tomó en esa reunión silenciosa y reservada.

Algunos dicen que Ethan Thorne fue liberado discretamente meses después en circunstancias misteriosas. Otros afirman que Vance rechazó la oferta, dejando a su hermano morir tras las rejas.

Pero una verdad perdura: Ethan Thorne vendió todo lo que había que vender: verdad, lealtad e incluso sangre.

Y al final, lo que compró fue la inmortalidad a las sombras de su propia leyenda.

Fin

III

The Neighborhood Watch

Written By R.K. Issacs Thomas Sr.

Nineteen

Chapter 1

The Perils of Order

Karen's life on Whispering Willow Lane was a constant, low-level military operation against disorder. She didn't call it racism; she called it maintaining standards. If the standards involved an aggressive focus on the new Black family, the Davises, that was simply because *they* seemed to generate the most... noise.

The kids. That was Karen's biggest daily grievance. Not just her usual targets—Zuri, the young Davis girl, who sometimes forgot to retrieve her brightly colored kickball from the sidewalk, or Elias, the teenage son, whose headphones, she swore, made his bass-heavy music vibrate through the pavement—but all the kids. They had an unnerving habit of existing loudly, and Karen saw it as a slow, corrosive attack on property values.

Her phone log was a testament to her vigilance.

- **June 14th, 3:45 PM:** Called about "excessive noise" (laughter during a sprinkler game).
- **July 3rd, 7:10 PM:** Called about "unsafe obstruction" (Elias Davis and his friend sitting on the curb).
- **August 1st, 11:00 AM:** Called about "suspicious activity" (Mr. Davis using a leaf blower on a Saturday morning, which Karen deemed too early).

The police knew her number. Officer Miller usually took the calls, his voice a flat, weary monotone. "Yes, ma'am, we'll send a unit to check on the... uh... activity." He'd learned that sending a unit usually meant the car would drive slowly past, and Karen would feel vindicated for another week.

The Davises, of course, were the main event. Anthony and Maya Davis had moved in with an air of quiet competence that Karen mistook for smugness. She had been raised by parents who operated on a clear, if unspoken, truth: **difference was disruption.** Her father, a man who believed in keeping his own lawn surgically perfect, had often warned her about "people who bring their chaos with them." Karen didn't hate the Davises; she simply believed they were genetically incompatible with the established, predictable tranquility of Whispering Willow Lane.

One Tuesday in late September, the daily aggravation reached its peak. Karen was enjoying her mid-morning surveillance when a rogue basketball bounded off her prize-winning azalea bush. It was the neighbor boy, Timmy, chasing it, but Karen didn't care. She stomped out onto her porch, pointing a stiff finger down the street.

"That's *it*!" she snapped, loud enough for Mrs. Davis, who was watering flowers across the street, to hear. "I'm calling the authorities! This constant harassment must stop!"

She marched inside, fuming, and dialed the precinct, giving her rehearsed, slightly breathless report about "unsupervised activity leading to property damage." She hung up feeling the familiar, righteous rush of a battle won. Her actions always led to a temporary, satisfying lull in the neighborhood's existence.

About an hour later, the police car drove past slowly and deliberately. Karen smiled a thin, pleased smile. Her efforts, often mocked by her more relaxed neighbors, were her safeguard. She was the watchtower, and eventually, her persistence would pay off.

She just didn't realize how terribly right she was.

The event unfolded that afternoon, right as the kids were getting off the school bus. Karen was wiping down her windowsill when a dark van—the kind she knew didn't belong—pulled up two doors down at the vacant Miller house. Two men in dark clothing, moving with unnerving speed, slipped toward the Davises' backyard.

Karen grabbed her ever-present binoculars, her initial thought being *they must be stealing a bicycle—I warned the police about this element!* But as the lenses focused, the glint wasn't off a bicycle handle; it was off something cold, long, and metallic. This was not a noise complaint.

A high-pitched, desperate cry ripped through the quiet street—Maya Davis's voice. The sound tore through Karen's sense of order like a physical blow. She saw a frantic struggle, a blurred push against a glass door, and then the sickening *smash* of the glass giving way.

For years, Karen had called the police on the Davis family for just existing. Now, as the true, horrifying violence unfolded before her, she did something she rarely did: she froze. Not out of fear, not yet, but out of a paralyzing recognition that her petty concerns had shielded her from the actual dangers lurking outside her world.

She watched the tragedy unfold: the hurried, vicious movements of the intruders, the desperate defense, and then the final, brutal silence as they fled.

When the sirens *finally* wailed, responding this time to an actual murder—the senseless killing of Elias Davis, the teenage boy she had only seen as a disruption—Karen dropped the binoculars. They hit the floor with a hollow thud.

The police arrived. The street was cordoned off. Maya Davis was rushed to the hospital, gravely injured but alive. Elias was gone. The family she had been raised to prejudge, the one she had called the police on multiple times for imagined offenses, was now the victim of a devastating, unimaginable crime.

When the detective approached her, Karen was rigid. She could recall the make of the van, the exact time the sun glinted off the weapon, and the specific torn corner of one man's jacket. Her meticulous, judgmental observation had paid off, but the price was seeing the true face of hatred.

In the sterile light of the interrogation room, the detective asked her to describe the Davises. Karen opened her mouth, intending to recount the "disruptions," the chaos she'd always seen. But the words that came out were very different.

"They were… they were always polite," she whispered, her voice cracking. "They kept their lawn nice. They were neighbors. I didn't see color when it happened, Detective. I only saw an innocent boy trying to save his mother."

The ingrained instruction from her mother and father—that unspoken code of racial dismissal—finally cracked. Her constant vigilance and her lifelong pursuit of order had culminated not in the banishment of difference, but in the witnessing of a universal truth: that a heart broken by loss looked exactly the same, regardless of skin color.

Twenty

Chapter 2

The State vs. The Accused: Witness Number Twelve

Karen's testimony, initially viewed with suspicion due to her frequent and frivolous calls, would become the final, unimpeachable warning which was the key evidence to convict the killers. Her journey from the prejudiced, petty neighbor to the reluctant, crucial witness had begun.

The air in the courtroom was thick, not just with the stale scent of wood and dust, but with palpable tension. Nearly six months had passed since the murder of Elias Davis. Maya Davis, miraculously recovering from her injuries, sat in the front row, a figure of quiet, heartbreaking resolve next to her husband, Anthony, and their daughter, Zuri.

The defendants, two men named Marcus Vale and Darryl Hynes, sat stone-faced at their table, radiating a cold indifference that made the hairs on the back of Karen's neck prickle.

Karen, formally known as Ms. Karen Periwinkle, was due to be the final and most crucial witness. The entire case—a tangle of circumstantial evidence, a lack of solid physical evidence at the scene, and a hesitant initial police response—hinged almost entirely on the one unlikely eye that had seen everything. This was the neighborhood's biggest busybody.

Twenty-One

Chapter 3

The Prosecution's Case: The Watchtower

When the Assistant District Attorney, Mr. Reynolds, called her name, a hush fell over the gallery. Karen walked to the stand with her back ramrod straight. She took the oath. She looked nothing like the "nosy neighbor" the defense was sure to paint. She looked like a woman carrying a terrible weight.

Mr. Reynolds began gently, guiding her through her history of civic duty—a subtle way of framing her vigilance as a positive trait.

"Ms. Periwinkle," Reynolds asked, standing near the jury box, "on the afternoon of September 22nd, what, precisely, drew your attention to the Davis home?"

Karen gripped the sides of the witness stand, her voice firm. "The van. A dark gray, late-model utility van with exceptionally dark, aftermarket window tint. It was backed up to the Miller property, two houses down from mine. It didn't belong."

"And why were you watching so closely?" She paused. This was the moment she had rehearsed for. "Because I always watch the street, Mr. Reynolds. I maintain a log of activity. I track what is normal and what is disorderly."

She then launched into a stunningly precise, minute-by-minute account of the break-in. "The first man, the taller one, Mr. Vale, was wearing a thick, black canvas jacket. It had a faded, stitched-on logo on the right shoulder—circular, with what looked like a stylized 'C.' The sleeve was torn near the elbow. I noted the tear was jagged, not clean."

"The second man, Mr. Hynes, had a distinct gait. He favored his right leg slightly, a very subtle hitch, as if compensating for an old injury. I saw him take three steps up Davis's deck; the first step was always shorter than the next two."

"The weapon used to break the glass—I saw the light hit it. It was a long-handled pry bar, chrome finish, with a slightly bent tip. When he dropped it, it made a particular metallic sound on the wooden deck."

Karen didn't just recall the events; she recalled the texture, the motion, the sound. Her obsessive cataloging of life on Whispering Willow Lane was now being used for its true purpose: justice. The jury—and especially the judge, Honorable Judge Thompson—watched her, their initial skepticism dissolving into awe.

Twenty-Two

Chapter 4

The Cross-Examination: The Poisoned Well

The defense attorney, a sleek, aggressive woman named Ms. Chavez, rose for the cross-examination with her purpose clear: to discredit Karen by highlighting her prejudice.

"Ms. Periwinkle," Chavez began, her tone dripping with saccharine disbelief. "You told the police you had called them numerous times about the Davis family prior to this incident, correct?"

"Yes," Karen stated, unflinching.

"You called them because the son, Elias, was sitting on the curb, which you reported as 'suspicious activity'?"

"I did."

"You called them because the Davises were having a barbecue, reporting 'excessive smoke'?"

"That is correct."

Ms. Chavez moved closer to the stand, her voice rising. "So, let's be honest, Ms. Periwinkle. You had a problem with the Davises because they were different. You had a problem with them because they were Black, didn't you? You prejudged them, you harassed them, and now you want this court to believe your biased eyes over your clearly biased history!"

The air crackled. The Davises shifted uncomfortably. Karen's past—the silent, inherited racism—was laid bare for the entire court. She had to answer, not just to the court, but to the ghosts of her parents.

Karen looked directly at Ms. Chavez, then past her to the jury. Finally, her gaze settled on Maya Davis, the grieving mother.

"Yes," Karen said, her voice dropping to a low, powerful register. "I judged them. I judged them unfairly, and yes, it was because of the way I was raised, because of the things I was told to believe about Black families and 'order' and 'chaos.' I was wrong. Terribly, unforgivably wrong." She paused, taking a breath that seemed to pull all the oxygen from the room.

"But when I saw those men break into their home, when I heard that boy scream and watched him fall… I didn't see a Black family getting what I secretly thought they deserved. I saw evil. I saw innocence being murdered. I saw a mother's life being shattered."

Karen leaned forward, her eyes blazing with conviction. "I memorized the logo, the limp, and the weapon because my gut told me that a boy's life mattered. And if I am a nosy, judgmental, and prejudiced woman, then let my terrible traits be used for the first time in my life to bring justice to the people I unjustly hated."

She finished her statement, and the courtroom was so silent that you could hear the quiet, audible sniffle of a juror. Karen's raw honesty—the acknowledgment of her own deep prejudice alongside her factually detailed eyewitness account—was overwhelming. She had stripped away her self-deception and presented the truth, warts and all. She had won the court over.

Twenty-Three

Chapter 5

The Verdict and the New Dawn

The jury deliberated for less than six hours. When they returned, the foreman's voice was clear: **Guilty** on all counts.

Justice Thompson delivered the sentence swiftly and decisively. Based on the brutality of the crime, the criminal history of the defendants, and the powerful evidence presented—evidence that relied almost entirely on Karen Periwinkle's testimony—Marcus Vale and Darryl Hynes were each sentenced to **50 Years to Life** in a state penitentiary.

As the judge concluded, Karen looked over toward the Davis family. Anthony Davis nodded to her, a gesture of profound, complicated respect. Maya Davis simply placed her hand over her heart and offered a faint, tearful smile.

Walking out of the courtroom, Karen felt lighter than she had in decades. She had been the Final Warning to the killers, and, more importantly, to herself.

That night, she sat in her kitchen, looking out the window. She no longer saw "disruption" or "disorder" when Zuri Davis came out to play. She saw a little girl who had lost her brother, now trying to live her life.

Karen realized her parents had not given her an understanding of the world; they had given her a prison. The true colors of the Davises—their dignity, their resilience, their love—had been revealed to her not through a lesson, but through a terrifying violent truth.

She finally understood that her parents' fear was not a guide to life, but a cage, and the key had been the simple, undeniable humanity she witnessed in the Davises' tragedy. Karen Periwinkle found a quiet kindness in her heart, finally understanding that the real true color of any individual was simply their humanity, not the pigment of their skin. Her lifelong prejudice was violently exposed and had finally begun to heal.

The End

IV

En Espanol

Twenty-Four

Capítulo 1

Los peligros del orden

La vida de Karen en Whispering Willow Lane fue una operación militar constante y de bajo nivel contra el desorden. Ella no lo llamaba racismo; lo llamaba mantener estándares. Si los estándares implicaban un enfoque agresivo en la nueva familia Black, los Davis, era simplemente porque parecían generar el más... ruido.

Los niños. Esa era la mayor queja diaria de Karen. No solo sus objetivos habituales—Zuri, la joven Davis, que a veces se olvidaba de recoger su balón de colores brillantes de la acera, o Elias, el hijo adolescente, cuyos auriculares, juraba, hacían vibrar su música con graves a través del asfalto—sino todos los niños. Tenían la inquietante costumbre de existir ruidosamente, y Karen lo veía como un ataque lento y corrosivo al valor de las propiedades.

Su registro de llamadas era un testimonio de su vigilancia.

- **14 de junio, 15:45:** Llamaron por "ruido excesivo" (risas durante un partido de aspersores).
- **3 de julio, 19:10:** Llamada por "obstrucción insegura" (Elias Davis y su amigo sentados en la acera).
- **1 de agosto, 11:00 AM:** Llamada por "actividad sospechosa" (el Sr. Davis usando un soplador de hojas un sábado por la mañana, que Karen consideró demasiado temprano).

La policía conocía su número. El agente Miller solía atender las llamadas, con voz monótona y cansada. "Sí, señora, enviaremos una unidad para comprobar la... eh... actividad." Había aprendido que enviar una unidad normalmente significaba que el coche pasaría despacio, y Karen se sentiría reivindicada durante otra semana.

Los Davis, por supuesto, eran el plato fuerte. Anthony y Maya Davis se mudaron con un aire de competencia tranquila que Karen confundió con arrogancia. Había sido criada por padres que operaban bajo una verdad clara, aunque no dicha: **la diferencia era la interrupción.** Su padre, un hombre que creía en mantener su propio césped quirúrgicamente perfecto, a menudo le advertía sobre "personas que traen su caos consigo." Karen no odiaba a los Davis; simplemente creía que eran genéticamente incompatibles con la tranquilidad establecida y predecible de Whispering Willow Lane.

Un martes a finales de septiembre, la molestia diaria alcanzó su punto máximo. Karen disfrutaba de su vigilancia a media mañana cuando un balón de baloncesto rebelde rebotó en su galardonada azalea ganadora. Era el chico vecino, Timmy, quien lo perseguía, pero a Karen no le importaba. Salió pisando fuerte al porche, señalando con un dedo rígido calle abajo.

"¡Eso es*!*" soltó, lo suficientemente alto para que la señora Davis, que regaba flores al otro lado de la calle, la oyera. "¡Voy a llamar a las autoridades! ¡Este acoso constante debe parar!"

Entró furiosa, y marcó la comisaría, entregando su ensayado y algo entrecortado informe sobre "actividad no supervisada que puede causar daños materiales". Colgó sintiendo la familiar y justa emoción de una batalla ganada. Sus acciones siempre provocaban una pausa temporal y satisfactoria en la existencia del barrio.

Una hora después, el coche de policía pasó despacio y con cuidado. Karen sonrió una sonrisa fina y satisfecha. Sus esfuerzos, a menudo objeto de burlas por sus vecinos más relajados, eran su salvaguarda. Ella era la torre de vigilancia y, al final, su persistencia daría sus frutos.

Simplemente no se daba cuenta de lo terriblemente acertada que estaba.

El evento se desarrolló esa tarde, justo cuando los niños bajaban del autobús escolar. Karen se limpiaba el alféizar cuando una furgoneta oscura—de esas que sabía que no encajaba—se detuvo dos puertas más abajo, en la desierta casa de los Miller. Dos hombres vestidos de oscuro, moviéndose a una velocidad inquietante, se deslizaron hacia el jardín trasero de los Davis.

Karen cogió sus eternos prismáticos, pensando *inicialmente que debían estar robando una bicicleta—¡avisé a la policía sobre este elemento!*

Pero al enfocar las lentes, el brillo no se reflejaba en el asa de una bicicleta; era en algo frío, largo y metálico. Esto no era una queja por ruido.

Un grito agudo y desesperado desgarró la calle silenciosa—la voz de Maya Davis. El sonido destrozó el sentido de orden de Karen como un golpe físico. Vio una lucha frenética, un empujón borroso contra una puerta de cristal y luego el nauseabundo *estruendo* del cristal cediendo.

Durante años, Karen había llamado a la policía por la familia Davis simplemente por existir. Ahora, mientras la verdadera y horrible violencia se desarrollaba ante ella, hizo algo que rara vez hacía: se quedó paralizada. No por miedo, todavía no, sino por un reconocimiento paralizante de que sus preocupaciones mezquinas la habían protegido de los peligros reales que acechaban fuera de su mundo.

Observó cómo se desarrollaba la tragedia: los movimientos apresurados y feroces de los intrusos, la defensa desesperada y luego el silencio final y brutal mientras huían.

Cuando las sirenas *finalmente* sonaron, esta vez respondiendo a un asesinato real—el asesinato sin sentido de Elias Davis, el adolescente que solo había visto como una interrupción—Karen dejó caer los prismáticos. Cayeron al suelo con un golpe seco.

Llegó la policía. La calle fue acordonada. Maya Davis fue trasladada de urgencia al hospital, gravemente herida pero viva. Elias se había ido. La familia a la que había sido criada para juzgar, a la que había llamado a la policía varias veces por delitos imaginarios, ahora era víctima de un crimen devastador e inimaginable.

Cuando el detective se acercó a ella, Karen estaba rígida. Recordaba la marca de la furgoneta, el momento exacto en que el sol brillaba en el arma y la esquina específica y desgarrada de la chaqueta de un hombre. Su observación meticulosa y crítica había dado resultado, pero el precio era ver la verdadera cara del odio.

A la luz estéril de la sala de interrogatorios, el detective le pidió que describiera a los Davis. Karen abrió la boca, con la intención de relatar las "interrupciones", el caos que siempre había visto. Pero las palabras que salieron fueron muy diferentes.

"Eran... siempre fueron educados", susurró, con la voz quebrada. "Mantenían bien el césped. Eran vecinos. No vi color cuando pasó, detective. Solo vi a un chico inocente intentando salvar a su madre."

La instrucción arraigada de su madre y su padre—ese código tácito de desprecio racial—finalmente se rompió. Su vigilancia constante y su búsqueda de orden de toda la vida no culminaron en el destierro de la diferencia, sino en el testimonio de una verdad universal: que un corazón roto por la pérdida se veía exactamente igual, independientemente del color de piel.

Twenty-Five

Capítulo 2

El Estado contra el acusado: Testigo número doce

El testimonio de Karen, inicialmente visto con sospecha debido a sus frecuentes y frívolas llamadas, se convertiría en la advertencia final e intachable que fue la prueba clave para condenar a los asesinos. Comenzó su camino de vecina prejuiciosa y mezquina a testigo reacia y crucial.

El aire en la sala del tribunal era denso, no solo con el olor rancio a madera y polvo, sino con una tensión palpable. Habían pasado casi seis meses desde el asesinato de Elias Davis. Maya Davis, recuperándose milagrosamente de sus heridas, estaba sentada en primera fila, una figura de silenciosa y desgarradora determinación junto a su marido, Anthony, y su hija, Zuri.

Los acusados, dos hombres llamados Marcus Vale y Darryl Hynes, estaban sentados con el rostro impasible en su mesa, irradiando una fría indiferencia que hacía que a Karen se le erizara el vello de la nuca.

Karen, conocida formalmente como la señorita Karen Periwinkle, iba a ser la testigo final y más crucial. Todo el caso—un enredo de pruebas circunstanciales, la falta de pruebas físicas sólidas en la escena y una respuesta inicial inicial vacilante—dependía casi por completo del único ojo improbable que lo había visto todo. Era el mayor entrometido del barrio.

Twenty-Six

Capítulo 3

El caso de la fiscalía: La Torre de Vigilancia

Cuando el fiscal adjunto, el señor Reynolds, la llamó, cayó un silencio sobre la sala. Karen caminó hasta el estrado con la espalda recta como un palo. Prestó juramento. No se parecía en nada a la "vecina entrometida" que la defensa seguramente iba a pintar. Parecía una mujer cargada con un peso terrible.

El señor Reynolds comenzó con suavidad, guiándola por su historia de deber cívico—una forma sutil de enmarcar su vigilancia como un rasgo positivo.

"Señorita Periwinkle", preguntó Reynolds, de pie cerca del estrado del jurado, "en la tarde del 22 de septiembre, ¿qué fue exactamente lo que llamó su atención hacia la casa de los Davis?"

Karen agarró los laterales del estrado, con voz firme. "La furgoneta. Una furgoneta utilitaria gris oscuro, modelo reciente, con un tinte de ventana excepcionalmente oscuro y de posventa. Estaba respaldada en la propiedad Miller, dos casas más allá de la mía. No pertenecía."

"¿Y por qué estabas observando tan de cerca?" Hizo una pausa. Este era el momento para el que había ensayado. "Porque siempre vigilo la calle, señor Reynolds. Llevo un registro de actividad. Registro lo que es normal y lo que es desordenado."

Luego comenzó a contar un relato asombrosamente preciso, minuto a minuto, del robo.

"El primer hombre, el más alto, el señor Vale, llevaba una chaqueta gruesa de lona negra. Tenía un logo descolorido y cosido en el hombro derecho—circular, con lo que parecía una 'C' estilizada. La manga estaba rota cerca del codo. Noté que el desgarro era irregular, no limpio."

"El segundo hombre, el señor Hynes, tenía un paso muy marcado. Inclinaba ligeramente la pierna derecha, un pequeño trozo muy sutil, como si compensara una vieja herida. Le vi dar tres pasos por la cubierta del Davis; el primer paso siempre era más corto que los dos siguientes."

"El arma usada para romper el cristal—vi cómo la luz le alcanzó. Era una palanca de mango largo, acabado cromado, con la punta ligeramente doblada. Cuando la dejó caer, hizo un sonido metálico particular en la cubierta de madera."

Karen no solo recordaba los hechos; recordaba la textura, el movimiento, el sonido. Su obsesiva catalogación de la vida en Whispering Willow Lane ahora se usaba para su verdadero propósito: la justicia. El jurado—y especialmente el juez, la Honorable Jueza Thompson—la observaban, su escepticismo inicial se disolvía en asombro.

Twenty-Seven

Capítulo 4

El contrainterrogatorio: El pozo envenenado

La abogada defensora, una mujer elegante y agresiva llamada Sra. Chávez, se presentó al contrainterrogatorio con su propósito claro: desacreditar a Karen destacando sus prejuicios.

"Señorita Periwinkle", comenzó Chavez, con un tono cargado de incredulidad empalagosa. "Le dijo a la policía que les había llamado numerosas veces sobre la familia Davis antes de este incidente, ¿correcto?"

"Sí", afirmó Karen, sin titubear.

"¿Les llamaste porque el hijo, Elias, estaba sentado en la acera, lo que denunciaste como 'actividad sospechosa'?"

"Sí."

"¿Los llamaste porque los Davis estaban haciendo una barbacoa, reportando 'humo excesivo'?"

"Eso es correcto."

La señorita Chavez se acercó al estrado, su voz subiendo en alto. "Seamos sinceros, señorita Periwinkle. Tenías un problema con los Davis porque eran diferentes. Tenías un problema con ellos porque eran negros, ¿verdad? Los prejuzgaste, los acosaste, y ahora quieres que este tribunal crea tus ojos parciales en lugar de tu historia claramente parcializada."

El aire chisporroteaba. Los Davis se movieron incómodos. El pasado de Karen—el racismo silencioso y heredado—quedó al descubierto ante toda la corte. Tenía que rendir cuentas, no solo ante la corte, sino ante los fantasmas de sus padres.

Karen miró directamente a la señorita Chávez, luego más allá de ella al jurado. Finalmente, su mirada se posó en Maya Davis, la madre afligida.

"Sí", dijo Karen, bajando la voz a un tono bajo y poderoso. "Los juzgué. Los juzgué injustamente, y sí, fue por la forma en que me criaron, por las cosas que me dijeron que creyera sobre las familias negras, el 'orden' y el 'caos'. Me equivoqué. Terriblemente, imperdonablemente equivocado."

Hizo una pausa, tomando aire que pareció absorber todo el olor de la habitación.

"Pero cuando vi a esos hombres irrumpir en su casa, cuando oí a ese chico gritar y lo vi caer... No vi a una familia negra recibiendo lo que en secreto pensé que merecían. Vi el mal. Vi a la inocencia ser asesinada. Vi la vida de una madre destrozada."

Karen se inclinó hacia adelante, con los ojos ardiendo de convicción. "Memoricé el logo, la cojera y el arma porque mi instinto me decía que la vida de ese chico importaba. Y si soy una mujer entrometida, crítica y prejuiciosa, que mis terribles rasgos se utilicen por primera vez en mi vida para hacer justicia a las personas a las que odiaba injustamente."

Terminó su declaración, y la sala estaba tan silenciosa que se podía oír el suave y audible sollozo de un jurado. La honestidad cruda de Karen—el reconocimiento de su propio profundo prejuicio junto a su relato de testigo presencial tan detallado—era abrumadora. Había despojado su autoengaño y presentado la verdad, con sus defectos y todo. Había conquistado el tribunal.

Twenty-Eight

Capítulo 5

El veredicto y el nuevo amanecer

El jurado deliberó durante menos de seis horas. Cuando regresaron, la voz del capataz era clara: **culpable** de todos los cargos.

El juez Thompson dictó la sentencia de forma rápida y contundente. Basándose en la brutalidad del delito, el historial criminal de los acusados y las pruebas contundentes presentadas—pruebas que se basaban casi en su totalidad en el testimonio de Karen Periwinkle—Marcus Vale y Darryl Hynes fueron condenados cada uno a **50 años a cadena perpetua** en una penitenciaría estatal.

Cuando el juez concluyó, Karen miró hacia la familia Davis. Anthony Davis asintió, un gesto de respeto profundo y complicado. Maya Davis simplemente se cubrió el pecho y le dedicó una leve sonrisa entre lágrimas.

Al salir de la sala, Karen se sintió más ligera que en décadas. Había sido la

Advertencia Final para los asesinos y, más importante aún, para sí misma.

Esa noche, se sentó en su cocina, mirando por la ventana. Ya no veía "disrupción" ni "desorden" cuando Zuri Davis salía a jugar. Veía a una niña pequeña que había perdido a su hermano, ahora intentando vivir su vida.

Karen se dio cuenta de que sus padres no le habían dado una comprensión del mundo; le habían dado una prisión. Los verdaderos colores de los Davis—su dignidad, su resiliencia, su amor—se le habían revelado no a través de una lección, sino mediante una verdad violenta y aterradora.

Por fin comprendió que el miedo de sus padres no era una guía para la vida, sino una jaula, y la clave había sido la humanidad simple e innegable que presenció en la tragedia de los Davis. Karen Periwinkle encontró una bondad silenciosa en su corazón, comprendiendo por fin que el verdadero color de cualquier individuo era simplemente su humanidad, no el pigmento de su piel. Su prejuicio de toda la vida quedó violentamente expuesto y por fin había comenzado a sanar.

Fin

V

Love of Justice and Love of Truth

Written By R.K. Issacs Thomas Sr.

Twenty-Nine

Chapter 1

The Hollow Echo

The silence in the apartment was the worst kind of souvenir. It was the echo of **Elias**, Stormy's father—a man whose life had been loud, full of bad jazz records and even worse jokes. Now, four months after the funeral, the silence was absolute and felt like a heavy quilt pressed over everything.

Stormy sat on the sofa while the light from the late afternoon sun failed to warm the chipped porcelain mug in her hands. She was twenty-two, freshly graduated, and suddenly adrift. Her father hadn't left her a grand inheritance, but he did leave her a small, rent-controlled apartment above the antique bookstore that he had managed, and a stack of unanswered questions about the car crash that had taken him.

The police had called it a reckless driving fatality where a drunk driver swerved and hit Elias's car head-on. The driver had survived, barely, and was now serving time in the low security correctional facility just outside the city limits. Stormy had tried to read the police reports, but the legal jargon blurred into incomprehensible noise. All she knew was the name: **Ethan Vance**.

A week ago, desperate to replace the hollow feeling in her chest with something purposeful, Stormy had accepted a part-time job as a clerk at the local Victim Services Outreach (VSO) office. It was a macabre irony, she knew. She was a victim herself, yet she was now assisting others to navigate the systems that had failed her.

Her first assignment, which she had both dreaded and strangely craved, was tomorrow.

It was an intake shift at the Riverbend Correctional Annex.

The Annex was less a prison and more a fortress of bureaucracy, all gray cinder block and razor wire that somehow still looked faded under the weak fluorescent lights. Stormy clutched her worn brown leather shoulder bag, and the vinyl VSO badge sticky against her blouse.

The guard at the desk was a man named Gaven with a mustache that looked like a permanent scowl stared at her ID until she started to fidget. "Vance," he muttered, handing back her identification. "You're doing the intake for Vance today." Stormy froze. "Ethan Vance?"

"Yeah. Parole eligibility assessment. Big meeting. You're just logging his profile documentation, nothing heavy. Don't worry, lady, the Annex is low security; these guys are just doing their time." Gaven waved her through the internal gate. "Hallway C, third door on the left."

Stormy's heart hammered a frantic rhythm against her ribs. She had read the name on paperwork for months, but to be physically in the same building as the man who killed her father felt like standing in a toxic cloud. She nearly turned back, but the memory of her father's empty chair at the kitchen table pushed her forward. *I just need to see him,* she thought, *to see the monster who did this.*

Hallway C was sterile and echoing. She found the intake room, a small space dominated by a heavy, metal table. A stack of files lay neatly waiting for her. She was early.

She opened the first file, and there he was: **Ethan Vance**. A mugshot—clean-shaven, intense eyes with a faint, almost shy dip at the corner of his mouth. He looked younger than she had expected, maybe twenty-five, and utterly unremarkable. Not a monster at all, just a person who made a choice and destroyed a life.

A heavy door slid open behind her. She jumped, quickly snapping the file shut. "Sorry," a deep voice said. "Didn't mean to startle you. You must be the new VSO clerk." Stormy turned. The man standing in the doorway was taller than she had imagined from the mugshot, built leanly, and wearing the standard-issue gray uniform. It was Ethan Vance.

His eyes, so intense, quiet eyes from the photo focused on her. They held a raw weight of sorrow that instantly contradicted the idea of a careless drunk driver.

"Yes," Stormy managed, her voice barely a whisper. "I'm Stormy." She intentionally omitted her last name, feeling a bizarre need to keep that secret locked away.

Ethan gave a slow, measured nod. "It's good to finally put a face to the service. They told me someone new was coming." He paused, his gaze dropping respectfully. "Thank you for being here." The simple courtesy was disorienting. Stormy had expected defiance, arrogance, or remorse, but not this quiet gratitude. He walked to the opposite side of the metal table and sat, his movements practiced and slow, as if every joint carried a heavy burden.

"I need to verify some basic information for your assessment, Mr. Vance," Stormy said, finding strength in the formality of her VSO role. She opened his folder again, avoiding the crime details. "Date of birth?" He answered clearly. As she logged the data, the silence in the room stretched and became less about the prison and more about the two people inhabiting it.

"Is Stormy your full name?" Ethan asked softly, interrupting her work.

Stormy looked up, startled by the personal query. "Yes. My father always said I was born during a terrible storm." A small, sharp pain pierced her chest at the mention of Elias. Ethan listened, not with pity, but with a deep, focused interest that made her feel seen for the first time since her father died.

"It suits you," he said. "It sounds strong."

His unexpected observation was a crack in the cold wall she had built around her grief. She realized, with a sickening jolt, that she had completely forgotten he was the reason she was grieving. She had forgotten, for a split second, that he was the killer.

"Let's stick to the form, Mr. Vance," she stated, her voice regaining its professional edge, though her hand trembled slightly on the pen.

But the seed was planted. Stormy had come to see a monster and instead found a man who listened, and who saw strength in her name.

Thirty

Chapter 2

The Project

Stormy returned to the Riverbend Annex two days later, armed with a fresh folder and a self-assigned mission. She had spent the intervening hours researching rehabilitation statistics, reading articles on recidivism, and convincing herself that her father, Elias, would have wanted her to help others find a better path. This was not about Ethan

Vance, the killer; this was about Stormy, the empathetic VSO worker, doing her job.

She didn't use the excuse of Ethan's parole assessment again. Instead, she fabricated a new, ongoing program designed for long-term inmates exhibiting significant remorse and potential for successful reintegration. Her supervisor, overwhelmed and trusting, simply signed off on the new documentation.

When she stepped back into the sterile intake room, Ethan was already waiting. He stood immediately when she entered, a gesture of respect she found both formal and charming.

"Stormy," he said, the sound of her name rolling off his tongue with a gentle familiarity that surprised her. "I wasn't sure you'd be back so soon."

"This is part of the new 'Reintegration Compass' program," she explained, smoothing down a non-existent wrinkle on her skirt. She kept her tone rigidly professional. "It involves regular one-on-one assessments. We need to focus on your coping mechanisms and future goals, Mr. Vance." He nodded seriously, taking his seat. "I understand. And please, just Ethan."

"Ethan," she conceded, the barrier between them slipping another notch.

The sessions began structured, based strictly on the VSO worksheets: *What are three major regrets? How do you cope with isolation? Describe your accountability for the event that led to your incarceration.*

Ethan's answers were stark and unwavering. He never minimized the accident. He spoke of that night by mentioning a few too many drinks at a lonely bar, the decision to drive, the sudden flash of light, and the horrifying silence afterward with a crushing clarity that sounded like genuine torment.

"It's not just the time I'm serving in here," he confessed during their third session, his eyes fixed on the tabletop. "It's the time that I've robbed from someone else. I took a life. That's the sentence I have to live with."

Stormy had prepared herself for this. She had rehearsed a clinical response about cognitive restructuring. Instead, she found herself leaning forward, driven by a raw empathy she hadn't known she possessed.

"Do you know anything about the man you... the man you hit?" she asked, her voice barely audible.

Ethan sighed; a heavy weight was lifted from his chest. "I know that his name was Elias and that he was a father. The police reports were clear. I pray for his family everyday, Stormy. It's a cheap kind of penance, I know, but it's all I have."

His genuine, palpable pain was a confusing counterpoint to her image of the reckless driver. Stormy felt a dizzying mixture of relief and guilt. She felt relief that he wasn't a monster and guilt that she was hiding her identity while harvesting his grief.

"We need to focus on your life after release," Stormy steered them back, reaching for control. "What skills can you develop here? What's the goal?"

"A second chance," Ethan said simply, looking up at her. "To be a man worthy of that chance. If I ever get out, I want to work with my hands. Carpentry. Something real. Something that builds instead of destroys."

Over the next few weeks, the VSO sessions morphed. The official worksheets were completed swiftly, and the remaining time was filled with conversation. Stormy learned that Ethan was an autodidact, devouring every book the prison library held. He was insightful, wryly humorous, and fiercely protective of the weaker inmates. She found herself sharing details of her own life: her struggles after her father's death, her love for old films, and her frustration with her aimless post-graduate life.

She never mentioned Elias by name, referring only to "the loss." Ethan, sensing the depth of her grief, offered quiet comfort.

"Losing a parent changes the axis of your world," he said once, sharing a story about his own mother's distant passing. "It's okay to feel lost. The silence they leave behind is deafening." He understood the silence and her grief. He didn't know that he was the cause of it, yet he was also the only person who seemed to truly validate it. The irony was a tight coil in her stomach, but the emotional reward of his attention was too addictive to give up.

One afternoon, as she was gathering her materials, Ethan stopped her. "Stormy, I know this is highly inappropriate, and I respect the boundaries of your job, but… seeing you every week, it's the only thing that feels real in here. You give me hope." Stormy looked at his earnest face, seeing past the gray uniform to the man who was becoming the most important person in her solitary life. Her fingers twitched. She wanted to reach out, to reassure him.

I am helping him reform, she rationalized, pushing down the rising panic about her secret. *He is a good man who made a terrible mistake. He deserves a second chance.* "Keep working on your carpentry skills, Ethan," she said, her voice softer than intended. "Keep reading. That's the best hope you have."

The door slid open, and the guard gave her the universal sign for *time to go*. As she walked out, the knot of deceit tightened. This was no longer just a VSO project; this was a relationship built on a foundation of shifting sand.

Thirty-One

Chapter 3

The Unlocking

The news arrived not in the antiseptic silence of the VSO room, but via a jarring, unexpected phone call from her supervisor, Mr. Harrison.

"Stormy, are you sitting down? Vance. Ethan Vance. He's going to be the poster child for your Reintegration Compass program." Stormy, who was filling out expense reports in the quiet VSO office, gripped the phone receiver so tightly her knuckles went white. "What about him, Mr. Harrison?"

"The board reviewed his case, your comprehensive reports, and his spotless conduct record. They accelerated his parole hearing. It was this morning. He's out. Conditional release, work furlough, the whole nine yards. Effective next Friday." Mr. Harrison's voice was buoyant, oblivious to the panic seizing Stormy's chest. "A miracle, Stormy! You achieved a miracle!"

She managed a choked, "That's... wonderful news," before hanging up, her mind was a dizzying rush of disbelief and terror.

Ethan. Free?

In the controlled environment of the Annex, she was the gatekeeper, the one who held the power of knowledge—her knowledge of his crime, her secret identity. Outside, in the real world, they would be two people as equals, with a deep connection built on her intentional lie. The lie felt suddenly huge, suffocating. She had exactly one week to decide. If she cut contact now, she could rationalize it as maintaining professional boundaries. She could pretend the intensity of their connection was just a side effect of the high-pressure VSO work. But the thought of never seeing him again, of letting the silence and grief return, sent a cold spike of loneliness through her.

Stormy went to the Annex that same evening, scheduling an emergency exit interview. Gaven, the guard, smiled faintly. "He's ready for you, miracle worker." Ethan was pacing the small room, his eyes shining with a mixture of awe and fear. When he saw her, he stopped, looking like a man who had suddenly forgotten how to breathe the free air.

"Stormy," he whispered, walking quickly to the table. "I don't know what to say. It's because of you. Your reports...your guidance...you made me believe there was something outside worth working for." "It was your effort, Ethan," she insisted, setting down her briefcase. She could feel the walls of her professional persona crumbling.

"No." He shook his head with earnestness radiating off him. "Before you, I was just counting minutes. Now... I'm counting days until I can prove to you and to myself that I can be the man you believed I could be. The one who builds instead of destroys." His use of the word "builds" echoed their earlier conversation. He had taken her abstract encouragement and forged it into a tangible, hopeful future. She felt an overwhelming rush of pride and affection, momentarily eclipsing the deadly secret between them.

She looked at him, really looked at him and the intense sorrow in his eyes, the slight way he held his hands as if still anticipating cuffs and the internal debate ended. Her father was gone. Ethan was here. He was reformed, changed, and loved her. She couldn't let go. Not now. "Ethan," she began, her voice low and shaky. "I… I know the protocols. I shouldn't. But I can't stop seeing you. Not now. Not when you're finally out." His face broke into a smile that was hesitant but full of joy that was wiping years of institutional despair away. "Stormy, I didn't dare ask. I know the rules. But I need you. I really do."

"You'll need a place to work, a job to report to," she said, quickly reverting to logistics to maintain control. "I know a place. The owner of the antique bookstore below my apartment building is looking for help with restorations and framing. Light carpentry. He's an old friend of my family."

This was her first major step across the line: arranging his work just feet away from her home. It was risky, but it gave her a means to see him constantly without formally crossing the VSO line.

"You're doing this for me?" Ethan asked, his voice thick with emotion.

"I'm doing this because you deserve a second chance, Ethan," she repeated, clinging desperately to the reform narrative.

The following Friday felt like a release day for Stormy as well. She waited in her apartment, watching from the window as a battered VSO van dropped Ethan off near the antique bookstore. He looked awkward in borrowed clothes; jeans and a light gray pullover but completely transformed. He settled into the small, subsidized room arranged by the bookstore owner, Mr. Peterson, a generous, slightly eccentric man who had adored Elias. Stormy spent the next few days monitoring his progress with meticulous anxiety. Ethan was true to his word as he worked long, arduous hours, dedicating himself to sanding, staining, and delicate frame repair.

Their relationship outside the prison felt like navigating a beautiful, fragile landscape. Their first official date was a quiet evening on the rooftop of her apartment building, overlooking the glittering cityscape.

"Look at that," Ethan murmured, his voice laced with wonder. "I haven't seen stars like that in five years."

Stormy sat beside him, their shoulders barely touching. "They're the same stars, Ethan. You just have the freedom to look up now." He reached for her hand, his palm rough and calloused from work. His touch sent a current of warmth through her, a warmth that finally began to thaw the cold shell of grief she had lived inside since her father's death. She squeezed his hand back, acknowledging the emotional commitment they had both made. It was during these unguarded moments that the relationship deepened rapidly. Stormy saw the kind, reflective man he had become. Ethan saw the compassionate woman beneath the professional armor.

A month later, when he first kissed her, it was a hesitant and tender meeting of lips that held years of pent-up longing. Stormy finally allowed herself to believe that this was not a terrible mistake. This was real. This was the only person who understood her loneliness, even if he was the reason for it.

The lie, however, festered. She had been introduced to Mr. Peterson as "Stormy Lee." Ethan knew her as Stormy. But the bookstore owner sometimes slipped. One rainy Tuesday, Mr. Peterson was showing Ethan a complicated restoration project. "This belonged to Elias, Stormy's father. Poor man, taken too soon." Ethan froze, his eyes widening. He looked at Stormy, who was nearby, arranging a shelf. "Elias? Your father's name was Elias?" Stormy's stomach plummeted. This was the moment. She had to address it, or the whole deception would crumble right then.

"Yes," she said, walking over, keeping her voice steady despite the seismic shift happening beneath her. "Elias Thompson. Why? Do you recognize the name, Ethan?" Ethan relaxed his shoulders, a slight furrow in his brow. "No, no. It just—it's a nice name. I thought you had mentioned it before, maybe." He gave a small, warm smile.

"My apologies. I've just been so focused on getting these pieces right." He had dismissed it. He didn't connect "Elias Thompson," the victim of his crime, with "Elias," the father of the woman he loved. The papers and reports had focused on the crime, the dates, the address, not the life. He was still focused on his own remorse, not the victim's biography. Stormy felt a wave of dizzying relief, followed instantly by profound shame. She had escaped the truth again. But she knew, deep down, that her luck wouldn't hold forever.

Thirty-Two

Chapter 4

Building a Life

The ensuing six months was the happiest Stormy had ever known. The apartment, once a tomb of Elias's memory and Stormy's isolation, became a home brimming with shared energy. Ethan moved in officially two months after his release. He brought little with him—a handful of books, a worn leather Bible—but his presence filled the space completely.

He was meticulously neat, almost obsessively so, a lingering effect of prison life. He never raised his voice. He treated Stormy with a quiet reverence, as if she were the most fragile and valuable thing he had ever encountered. Their love wasn't wild or tumultuous; it was a steady current of devotion.

On Friday nights, after Mr. Peterson's bookstore closed, Ethan would clear the small kitchen table and teach Stormy the basics of joinery, demonstrating how to fit pieces of wood together seamlessly, locking them into an unbreakable bond. "That's what we're doing, Stormy," he'd say, sanding the rough edges of a small jewelry box he was making for her. "We're taking all these rough pieces like my past, your grief and finding the precise angles where they fit together. We're making something new and solid."

Ethan's rehabilitation was genuine. He volunteered his off-hours repairing homes for the elderly in the neighborhood. His hands, once used to driving carelessly, now dedicated to fixing and building. He wrote letters of apology to the judge and the probation officer, expressing deep gratitude for his second chance. Stormy watched him, her heart swelling with an emotion that was part love, part pride, and part profound, sickening guilt. He was the man she had helped create, the reformed soul she had fought for. How could this gentle, devoted person be the same man who shattered her world?

The truth of the crime became a phantom. In the daylight of their life together, it seemed impossible that Ethan could be the same person named in the cold police file. She had successfully compartmentalized: there was Ethan Vance, the kind, loving carpenter, and there was Ethan Vance, the incarcerated offender. She refused to let the two overlap each other. Their dates were simple: picnics by the city lake, browsing forgotten sections of the public library, and long discussions about books and philosophy. Stormy found herself laughing easily, genuinely, for the first time since her father's death. Ethan had given her life back its axis.

When they argued, it was always minor, usually about his insistence on taking responsibility for every single task, born of his fear of failing her or losing the life they had built. One evening, they were talking about future travel, and Stormy casually mentioned taking a road trip across the West Coast. Ethan's face immediately clouded over.

"No," he said, his voice flat. "I don't think I can do that, Stormy." "Why not?" He gripped his water glass tightly. "I won't drive long distance. I can't. I won't ever put myself in a position where I could repeat that mistake. Even if I'm sober, even if I'm careful. I just won't."

It was a stark, painful reminder. His inability to drive was a physical manifestation of his immense, ongoing guilt over the accident that killed her father. Instead of driving her away, his fear cemented her belief in his reform. He was punishing himself daily; he truly was a different man.

"Okay," Stormy said gently, placing her hand over his, "then we'll take trains. Or I'll drive. We'll figure it out. The point is being together." The commitment deepened naturally. They navigated holidays together. They shared a quiet, poignant Christmas, marked by Ethan's thoughtfulness in creating small, hand-carved gifts. They met Stormy's few remaining college friends, who, while initially skeptical of the 'ex-con' story, were quickly won over by Ethan's humble, attentive demeanor.

One blustery Saturday morning in early spring, Ethan insisted on hiking to the top of the nearby city reservoir overlook. It was chilly, but the view of their small city spread out below them was breathtaking. Ethan was unusually quiet on the ascent. When they reached the peak, he led her to a small, private ledge sheltered by pine trees. He didn't drop to one knee in the cinematic way; instead, he stood facing her, his intense eyes holding hers. From his pocket, he produced a small, velvet-lined box. Inside was a ring he had crafted himself. It was a simple silver band inlaid with a piece of dark, reclaimed wood, polished to a mirror sheen.

"This wood," he said, holding it carefully, "is salvaged from an old church bench. It's seen a lot of failure, a lot of grace, and a lot of quiet, persistent hope." His voice was rough with emotion. "Stormy, you saved my life. You rebuilt me. You gave me more than a second chance; you gave me a reason to be worthy of it. I know my past is dark, but my future is only bright if you're standing in it. Marry me."

Tears streamed down Stormy's cheeks. They were tears of joy, and tears of profound, terrible guilt. She looked at the earnest, wonderful man standing before her, a man who had admitted his crime and was working tirelessly to redeem himself, who loved her without reservation. She ignored the voice of her father's memory whispering in the back of her mind.

"Yes," she choked. "Yes, Ethan, I will marry you." He slid the ring onto her finger, and for a moment, the fit felt impossibly perfect. He wrapped her in a hug so fierce it nearly cracked her ribs, a physical manifestation of his fear and love. As they walked down the mountain holding hands, Stormy felt an exhilarating, reckless joy. She was engaged to the most incredible man she had ever met. The wedding was set for six months away—a beautiful, autumn ceremony. The wedding planning began immediately, consuming all their free time and reinforcing their commitment. They were a team, planning their future, cementing the lie deeper into the foundation of their life.

While Stormy and Ethan are wedding dress shopping, they run into Mark, a former colleague of Elias, who recognizes Ethan Vance's face from the high-profile crash reports. Mark publicly reveals to Ethan that Stormy is Elias Thompson's daughter. The revelation shatters Ethan, who sees her love as a calculated act of control and revenge. He rejects her and flees the city, seeking an honest, solitary penance.

Ethan retreats to the bookstore workshop. Stormy confesses her entire deception to Mr. Peterson, who offers counsel but confirms her fears that she compromised Ethan's true redemption. Ethan gives Stormy the ring back, refusing reconciliation, stating he cannot live a life built on a lie and that he must earn his truth alone. He leaves for a forestry job in the Rockies.

Thirty-Three

Chapter 5

The Weight of Memory

Stormy was a vessel emptied of sound and purpose. She sat in the middle of the living room floor, the sunlight filtering through the curtains illuminating the dust motes dancing in the air—the same dust motes she and Ethan had often watched together. Now, the apartment was a museum of their failure.

She picked up a worn, leather-bound hymnal from the coffee table, a relic of her childhood. The pages were thin, marked with her mother's elegant handwriting and underlined passages. The memory of her father, Elias, a single parent, and the profound role of the church in their lives, washed over her.

Her mother, Maria, had been a gentle, luminous woman whose life had been a testament to faith and devotion. She died giving birth to Stormy. The tragedy was not a lingering illness, but a sudden, violent loss that marked the beginning of Stormy's life with an immediate, deep void. Elias had never remarried. He had dedicated himself wholly to raising his daughter as a living memorial to his wife. "Your mother gave me the greatest storm and the greatest light," Elias used to tell her, touching her cheek with his rough carpenter's hand. He was often quiet, haunted by the absence of his wife, but he poured every ounce of his love into Stormy.

Their life was anchored by the church. It was a small, historic parish downtown where Maria had served as a Sunday school teacher. For Elias, faith wasn't a choice; it was a sustaining force. He and Maria had instilled in Stormy a fierce moral compass: one rooted in absolute honesty, penance for mistakes, and the unwavering belief that truth, no matter how painful, was the path to God's grace. "We are Thompson people," Elias would say, referencing her family name, which she had withheld from Ethan. "And Thompson people don't deal in shadows, Stormy. We stand in the light, even when it burns."

This deep, shared history was the source of Stormy's deepest pain and her most agonizing moral conflict. Elias wasn't just a father; he was her entire world, the sole guardian of her identity and the keeper of her mother's memory. When he died, the axis of her world not only shifted, but it vanished. The loss of Elias hadn't just taken a father; it had taken her partner in faith, the one person who truly understood the depth of her legacy. Her grief, therefore, was not merely sadness; it was a desperate, existential loneliness.

The realization that struck her now, sitting in the ruins of her relationship with Ethan, was the depth of her moral betrayal. By pursuing Ethan, she hadn't just lied to him; she had lied to the memory of her mother, betrayed the teachings of her father, and desecrated the principles of honesty that their faith demanded. Her relationship with Ethan, the man who was now trying to find his own honest path in the mountains, was the deepest shadow she had ever cast. She had encouraged him to seek redemption while she herself was swimming in a sea of deceit.

He took a life, she thought, pressing the hymnal to her chest. *And I took his truth.* Ethan's pain was amplified because he understood the true weight of sin and redemption, a weight like the spiritual foundation she had been raised on. He had sought grace through honesty and hard work; she had offered him a reprieve built on a terrible, fragile secret. If Elias had been alive, he would have demanded justice and honesty. If Maria had been alive, she would have offered forgiveness, but only through confession. Stormy had offered neither. She had simply buried the truth under the weight of her love.

The weight of her father's solitary struggle to raise her, his devotion to her mother's memory, and his sudden, violent end all coalesced into an overwhelming pressure. She didn't just need Ethan; she needed him to validate her life, to fill the gaping hole left by the loss of the only two people who had ever truly loved her.

The moral foundation, once so solid, was crumbling beneath her. Stormy realized that the choice wasn't just between **Love or Justice**; it was between **Love or Truth**. She had chosen love built on a lie, and now she had lost both. It was this despair, this profound sense of failing her own moral legacy, that gave her the reckless energy to seek answers where she hadn't before. If she couldn't have Ethan, she could at least restore her father's integrity and, perhaps, find a path to her own forgiveness. Driven by a desperate need to stand back in the light, she pushed the hymnal away and walked toward the small, locked box where she kept her most painful, guarded possessions: the original police reports on Elias Thompson's fatal crash.

Thirty-Four

Chapter 6

The Hidden Detail

Stormy opened the box. The police reports, the witness statements, and the vehicular homicide file were exactly as she had left them. She considered them to be stiff, cold, and impersonal. She had always avoided reading the details too closely, preferring the abstract horror of the crime to the painful specifics.

Now, she read every line, driven by a perverse desire to find something, anything, that might lessen Ethan's guilt or, selfishly, justify her lie. The reports detailed the accident: Elias Thompson was driving his sedan eastbound on Route 17 after a late night managing the bookstore. Ethan Vance was driving his pickup westbound, swerving across the center line after consuming a large quantity of alcohol. Head-on collision. Unambiguous. Yet, as she read, one detail, previously overlooked in her grief and hurry had snagged her attention: a marginal note in the traffic reconstructionist's report. It referred to a secondary witness, an anonymous motorist who had followed Elias Thompson's car for several miles just prior to the crash.

The witness stated that Mr. Thompson's sedan had been "driving erratically" and had briefly veered into the breakdown lane before correcting sharply, moments before the collision. The police had dismissed the observation, attributing Elias's movement to typical midnight fatigue, especially given Ethan Vance's undisputed intoxication.

But Stormy knew her father. Elias was a meticulous man, almost to a fault. He had never been reckless. However, a separate inventory log caught her eye: among Elias's effects found at the scene was a small, unopened bottle of prescription pain medication in his glove compartment. The prescription dated back several months, given for a flare-up of chronic back pain.

The reports confirmed a standard toxicology screen had been performed on Elias. She had never asked about the results and was only focusing on Ethan's BAC. She scanned the final page of the forensic inventory until she found the section: "Victim's Toxicology Results: Negative for alcohol. Trace amounts of prescription analgesic (Hydrocodone) detected. Below therapeutic threshold."

Below therapeutic threshold? It meant he wasn't impaired according to the letter of the law.

But a cold dread settled in Stormy's stomach. Her father had always refused to take those pills because they made him drowsy. Had he taken one late that night? Had the medication, combined with his fatigue, caused the momentary "erratic driving" the witness described? Had Ethan Vance, drunk and speeding, swerved into Elias, or had Elias briefly veered into the path of Ethan's oncoming truck?

The collision was still Ethan's fault—his intoxication was the proximate cause. But the crash suddenly looked less like a monstrous, unilateral crime and more like a catastrophic meeting of two errors: one drunk and one drowsy.

If there was even a fractional, tiny degree of fault on her father's side, it changed everything. It meant Ethan Vance hadn't murdered an innocent saint. It meant his crime, while terrible, was less the act of a purely destructive monster and more the tragic result of a systemic failure, one that involved her father's own lapse in judgment.

This small, hidden detail was not absolution, but it was a crucial complication. It was a pinprick of moral gray that might just be enough to save Ethan from the crushing weight of singular guilt he was carrying. It was a guilt she had exploited.

She realized what she had to do. She had to take the full weight of her deception and her father's hidden frailty and present it to Ethan, not to win him back, but to finally be honest with him. To confess the truth of her love and the new, terrible truth of the accident before he disappeared forever.

Thirty-Five

Chapter 7

The Final Confrontation

Stormy found Ethan where she knew he would be, which was in the small, borrowed apartment above the bookstore, boxing his few possessions. The room was nearly bare, holding only the scent of sawdust and the sharp, clean air of finality. He didn't look up when she entered.

"I need five minutes, Ethan," she said, her voice steady now, devoid of the pleading she'd used before. "And I need you to listen with an open heart, not the cynical one I created."

He paused, holding a heavy copy of The Count of Monte Cristo. "The open heart died in the bridal shop, Stormy." She ignored the barb. She walked to the small table and spread out the police files, the traffic reconstructionist's notes, and the toxicology report.

"This is not about the lie that I told you", She began, pointing to the sections. "It's about the lie you've been telling yourself to survive, and the one my family has been telling to mourn. I know you're guilty, Ethan. I know you were drunk, and you crossed the line. But I also found this." She tapped the two reports: the anonymous witness's mention of Elias driving "erratically," and the note about the trace amounts of Hydrocodone.

"My father," Stormy continued, her voice catching on a sudden wave of complicated grief, "was a good man, but he was struggling with pain and fatigue. He took pills he shouldn't have, and he was veering just before impact. It wasn't just your mistake, Ethan. It was a terrible, cosmic collision of two people making bad choices on a dark road."

Ethan finally looked at the papers, his brow furrowed, then at her. His face was a roadmap of confusion and deep, fresh pain. "You're trying to excuse me," he accused, his voice rough. "You're trying to shift the blame to your own father to keep me here."

"No," Stormy said, pushing the reports toward him. "I'm telling you the truth so you can finally be truly redeemed. You don't have to carry the entire, singular weight of being a murderer of an innocent. You carry the weight of being reckless. You carry the weight of taking a life, yes, but not the weight of being a monster." She stood up, folding her hands. "I am the daughter of the man you hit. And I am hopelessly in love with the man you became. I don't care if you're the killer; I just care that you're honest. If you stay, we will rebuild. Not on a lie, but on two broken people who are accountable for their choices."

Ethan slowly gathered the reports, his hands trembling as he stared at the toxicology notes. The information was a tiny, cold comfort, and a sliver of gray in the absolute blackness of his guilt. "I can't stay, Stormy," he said finally, his voice thick with sorrow. "Even with this... I need to earn my forgiveness in solitude. I need to prove to myself that the man you fell in love with is the man I can be when no one is watching."

He looked at her, his love undeniable, but tempered by an absolute moral necessity. "You lied to me. I took your father. We are poison to each other right now. This information is for you, Stormy. It's for your peace with Elias. But it doesn't change what I must do." He picked up his small travel bag.

"I will find you again," he promised, his eyes intense. "But only when I have rebuilt a foundation that is honest and whole. I will not come back until I know I deserve your love." He walked out, leaving Stormy standing alone amid the wreckage of his departure and the cold, new reality of her father's flawed innocence. The truth was out, but the love was gone, delayed by penance and broken trust.

Thirty-Six

Chapter 8

The Serpent in the Details

Ethan's absence left a wound that Stormy could no longer ignore or try to patch over with affection. Her period of penance was swift and painful. She quit the VSO job, offering a cryptic, honest-enough explanation to Mr. Harrison about a "profound ethical failure" related to a recent case. She sold the apartment, unable to stand the oppressive silence of a place that had housed her greatest love and her greatest deceit.

The engagement ring—the salvaged wood and silver band—remained on her finger, no longer a symbol of hope but a heavy reminder of her accountability. She was living simply now, renting a small room above a dry cleaner and dedicating her time to researching the final days of her father's life. She had to know the full truth of the crash, not just the partial truth she had presented to Ethan. She re-read the files hundreds of times, until the legal jargon blurred, searching for any detail that pointed away from the accident.

One evening, while comparing photos of the accident scene, she noticed an anomaly. The police photos showed Elias's car—a sedan—completely totaled on the driver's side, but one object was curiously preserved: the antique silver keychain he always carried, lying near the wreck. It held the keys to his sedan and the bookstore. The keychain was ornate, shaped like an old-fashioned compass.

She remembered the witness report stating Elias had "corrected sharply" right before the impact. Why would he have veered? Stormy went to Mr. Peterson at the antique bookstore, seeking comfort and information. He looked older now, weighed down by the knowledge of Stormy's secret and Ethan's quiet departure. "He called Stormy," Peterson said quietly, running a rag over a restored desk. "Ethan. He's working for a forestry service near the Rockies. He's safe.

He said he's paying his debt through honest work." "I know," Stormy replied, pulling out the faded accident photos. "But the debt isn't just to Elias, Mr. Peterson. It's the truth." She pointed to the photo of the silver compass keychain. "Did you ever notice anything strange about this? Right after the funeral, before I took the keys, did it look damaged?"

Peterson frowned, leaning closer. "The compass? No, it was fine. Elias cherished that. He said it kept him 'going true north,' whatever that meant. He had it fixed just a few weeks before... before the crash."

"Fixed?" Stormy asked, her heart hammering. "What was wrong with it?" Peterson thought for a moment. "It was rattling, he said. He took it to a repairman down on 5th Street, a locksmith. He said the housing around the needle was loose. Why?" Stormy didn't answer. She knew her father's meticulous nature. If the compass was loose, he would have had it repaired immediately. But what if the "rattling" wasn't a repair issue, but something placed inside? The next day, she tracked down the locksmith on 5th Street. The man, old and weary, barely remembered the repair. But when Stormy produced the photo of the compass, his memory cleared.

"Ah, the compass. Mr. Thompson. Nice man. He thought the needle housing was rattling loose. But it wasn't the housing." The locksmith leaned in, lowering his voice conspiratorially. "I found something inside the hollow space where the hinge should have been. It wasn't the hinge. It was a tiny, foreign object." "What kind of object?" Stormy urged, leaning over the counter.

"A chip," the man said, lowering his voice further. "A tiny black microchip, like something out of a phone. I took it out and put it in a tiny, taped-up envelope and showed it to him. He got this look on his face, pale as a ghost. He said, 'That's it. That's the reason.' He paid me double and told me to forget I ever saw it."

Stormy felt the blood drain from her face. A microchip. Something Elias felt was important enough to pay a locksmith to remove discreetly, and important enough to prompt the comment, *"That's the reason." A microchip is a tracking device.*

The terrifying realization struck her with the force of the collision itself. Elias wasn't just driving erratically because of medication and fatigue. He was being tracked. The witness account of Elias "veering sharply" suddenly took on a sinister new meaning. He hadn't just swerved out of fatigue; he had likely realized he was being followed or chased. He was trying to lose whoever was tracking him. And the head-on collision? It wasn't just a drunk driver making a fatal error. Ethan Vance's truck was simply in the wrong place at the right time for someone who wanted Elias Thompson dead.

Stormy raced back to her rented room, pulling out the files again. She found the police photo of Ethan's battered pickup truck. The front was smashed in from the head-on impact. But she noticed a tiny, almost imperceptible scratch mark on the passenger side mirror of Ethan's truck—a faint scrape that looked suspiciously like a secondary, glancing impact. An impact that would have occurred moments *before* the head-on crash, possibly from another vehicle attempting to run Elias off the road and into Ethan's path. The death of Elias Thompson was not an accident. It was an assassination orchestrated to look like a drunk driving fatality. And Ethan Vance, the man who had struggled with the overwhelming weight of being a killer, was nothing more than an unwitting pawn used to complete the murder. He was not the cause of Elias's death, but an accessory to the murder. He was used and destroyed by a hidden hand. Stormy's mission instantly changed. This wasn't about seeking personal redemption or saving a troubled man; it was about exposing a deadly conspiracy, clearing the name of the man she loved, and bringing true justice to the memory of her father. She had to find Ethan and tell him the truth.

Thirty-Seven

Chapter 9

The New Truth

The coordinates provided by Mr. Peterson led Stormy deep into the Montana Rockies, to a small, isolated camp run by a non-profit forestry service. It was a place of endless pine and granite, where the air was cold and clean, and the sky felt closer than the ground.

She found Ethan not in the camp office, but on a trail that was miles from civilization, wearing utilitarian work gear. His face was shaded by a wide-brimmed hat. He was leaning against a massive tree trunk while using his callused hands working a rough block of cedar with a small, sharp knife, carving the wood into an intricate, abstract shape. His penance, she realized, was perpetual.

She approached him silently, the crunch of her boots on the dry pine needles announcing her presence only moments before she reached him. Ethan's knife froze mid-stroke. He looked up, and the shock in his eyes was instant and profound, followed immediately by the familiar, weary resentment. "Stormy," he said, his voice husky, roughened by disuse. He didn't stand, didn't smile, and didn't move the knife. "You shouldn't be here."

"I know," she replied, her breath catching in her throat, not from the hike, but from the raw intensity of seeing him again. He was leaner, rougher, but the integrity she had fallen in love with radiated from him like a physical heat. She still wore the wooden ring. "I came because I found a new lie." Ethan scoffed, turning back to his carving. "I have no more capacity for lies, Stormy. Yours or mine."

"It's not ours," she insisted, taking a step closer. "It belongs to the person who set us up. Ethan, you weren't the cause of my father's death. You were the weapon." She reached into her backpack and pulled out the manila envelope containing the police report printouts, the locksmith's business card, and her own annotated photos. She didn't hand them to him; she needed him to hear the truth first, unfiltered by cynicism.

"My father, Elias, was being tracked. Not by the police, but by someone else," she revealed, detailing the compass, the microchip, and the locksmith's testimony. She then pointed to the photo of his truck. "The police missed it. They were looking for alcohol and speed. They missed the secondary scrape on your passenger mirror. I believe someone was forcing Elias off the road, pushing him directly into your path to make it look like a clear-cut drunk driving fatality."

Ethan finally dropped the knife. It fell silently into the pine needles. He stared at the reports, then at Stormy, his disbelief slowly morphing into a white-hot understanding. "The erratic driving… the Hydrocodone," he muttered, his mind rapidly re-processing his own memories of that night. "I remember a flicker. A sudden light behind the sedan, not just headlights. I thought it was the drinks playing tricks. But… if someone else was involved…"

The immense, crippling guilt he had carried for five years—the shame of being a *killer*— was being peeled away, replaced by the bitter, clarifying shock of being a pawn.

He looked at her, his eyes now blazing, not with anger at her, but with a fierce, directed rage at the unseen enemy. "I killed a man, Stormy. I was still drunk. That is my fault. But I didn't *murder* him. I didn't *initiate* the crash." "Exactly," she confirmed, relief washing over her that he wasn't rejecting the evidence, only the idea of their relationship. "You were used. The person who tracked Elias knew you were on that road, knew you were drunk, and knew your mistake would be the perfect cover for murder."

The air between them changed instantly. The wall of moral alienation collapsed, replaced by a common enemy and a shared, vital goal. The conflict was no longer *us vs. my father's memory*; it was *us vs. the real killer.*

Ethan stood up. He didn't reach for her, but for the cedar block and his knife, but this time, he tucked the knife safely away. "Who was tracking your father? Why?" "I don't know," Stormy admitted. "Elias was just a bookstore manager. But he was meticulous. He was secretive about the chip. He was hiding something, Ethan. Something worth killing for!" He finally looked at the engagement ring on her finger, and this time, the look held no bitterness. "You came all this way. You put yourself at risk. You told me the truth, finally." "I told you the truth because I love you," she stated simply. "And I refuse to let the real killer win twice by taking my father and by destroying the only honest man I've ever known." Ethan stepped closer, wiping the sawdust from his hands. Their eyes met, and in that moment, the romantic relationship was secondary. What mattered was the bond of absolute, terrifying trust.

"We don't rebuild on love, Stormy," he said, the words echoing their last conversation. "We rebuild on justice. We clear my name, and we bring the real killer to justice."

He reached out and gently squeezed her hand, resting his thumb on the wooden ring. "You just gave me my second chance back. Not my life, but my truth. Tell me where we start."

Thirty-Eight

Chapter 10

Putting It All Together

Stormy and Ethan drove back from the mountains without stopping, fueled by coffee and a burning urgency. They were no longer lovers in denial, but partners bound by danger and the pursuit of justice. They went straight to the antique bookstore. Mr. Peterson, stunned but deeply relieved to see Ethan, readily let them into the closed shop.

"Elias wasn't just managing the store," Stormy stated, sweeping her gaze across the dark wood and glass. "He was hiding something here, something worth killing for. The compass chip proves he was tracked. He veered to shake the tracker, and the killer forced him into Ethan's truck to cover their tracks." "The answer isn't in the new pieces," Ethan deduced, his mind sharp, his carpentry skills providing a new lens. "It's in the old ones. Elias did a lot of restoration work. If he was hiding something, he would integrate it into the wood. Where did he keep his tools right before...?"

Peterson pointed to a wall of old, unlabeled furniture that Elias had been personally restoring for a long-term client. "He was obsessed with that display case. Spent all his time on the joinery. Said he needed to make it 'invisible.'" Ethan went straight to the tall, mahogany display case. He didn't use a crowbar; he ran his hands along the corners, feeling for discrepancies in the wood grain that only a craftsman would know. His fingers paused on a seemingly seamless seam near the base.

"He used a butterfly joint here," Ethan muttered, his voice tense. "The strongest bond, meant to be permanent. But he engineered a hairline release." Working with two slim metal picks, Ethan bypassed the joint. A panel slid open, revealing a hidden compartment lined with velvet. Inside wasn't a jewel or a memory card, but a small, worn, leather-bound journal.

Stormy snatched the journal, flipping through the pages. It wasn't Elias's daily thoughts; it was a meticulous log. Dates, times, locations, and codes. She recognized one name immediately: Harrison.

The journal revealed that Elias hadn't just been tracking the *antique* collection; he had been logging the movements of a high-level fence who used the store as a laundering front. Elias had realized this fence was manipulating specific parole/rehabilitation programs to recruit recently released inmates for their operation—inmates whose desperation made them vulnerable. A name was circled repeatedly: Mr. Harrison.

"Harrison," Stormy whispered, the name of her VSO supervisor—the man who signed off on her fabricated program, the man who called Ethan's release a "miracle." "He didn't just sign off on your release, Ethan," Stormy realized, her face pale. "He targeted you. He saw your remorse, your carpentry skills, and your isolation. He manipulated your VSO file to get you a quick release, put you in the apartment building he controlled, and used Mr. Peterson as a cover for a job. He was grooming you to join his organization."

Ethan's face hardened with cold clarity. The initial remorse he felt for being drunk was now completely overshadowed by the deliberate malice of his true enemy. "The VSO program was a recruitment tool. He wasn't tracking Elias; he was tracking the *microchip*. Elias must have copied the operation's logistics, perhaps from the VSO files, onto a chip."

"Elias found out Harrison was using his store and his daughter's grieving city to run a criminal enterprise," Stormy concluded. "He took the chip, put it in his keychain to hide it, and Harrison realized Elias was the leak. The crash was Harrison neutralizing the threat and eliminating the witness, using the man he was trying to recruit as the perfect, disposable cover."

The journal had one final entry: a meeting time and location, scrawled hastily in the margin: *Tuesday, 10 PM. Riverbend Annex, main yard.* A date set for tomorrow night. "It's a security exchange," Ethan said, tapping the entry. "Harrison must have thought Elias was going to reveal the chip or use the information. He must go there regularly." Stormy looked at Ethan, the fierce love and shared purpose overcoming all the past pain. "He framed you once, Ethan. He won't get a second chance. We go to Riverbend tomorrow night. We give him the only thing he wants—this journal—and we get the truth."

"We use the same lie he built," Ethan agreed, his hand settling firmly over hers. "We lure him into the open."

Thirty-Nine

Chapter 11

The Riverbend Reckoning

The Riverbend Correctional Annex was quieter at night, shrouded in shadows that softened the razor wire and the harsh gray cinder block. The meeting was set for 10 PM in the staff parking lot, a place of constant surveillance but limited traffic after hours.

Stormy and Ethan were parked across the street, watching. They had made one call, not to the police yet, but to Mr. Peterson, who was waiting in a nearby café, ready to dial 911 at a pre-arranged signal. They needed Harrison's full confession on the record, not just the circumstantial evidence of the chip and the journal.

"He won't trust me," Stormy whispered, her hands gripping the steering wheel. "He knows I exposed myself. He'll expect a trap."

"He doesn't have a choice," Ethan replied, his voice a low, steady rumble. He was wearing the same borrowed clothes he'd worn the day of his release, a silent statement of his honest redemption. "Elias's journal is too valuable. It compromises his entire operation. Harrison needs to eliminate the journal and the two people who've read it."

Stormy had texted Harrison an hour ago: *I have the information that Elias Thompson was holding. Meet me at Riverbend Annex lot, alone. I want an explanation before I go public.*

Precisely at 10 PM, a sleek, unmarked black sedan pulled into the parking lot. Mr. Harrison emerged, looking impeccably professional in a dark suit, his face calm but his eyes sharp and calculating. He held a small, black case. Stormy got out of the car alone, carrying the leather journal openly. Ethan remained hidden, ready to intervene if the conversation turned dangerous—which they knew it would.

"Stormy. I had hoped our relationship could have ended without this drama," Harrison said, his tone was one of paternal disappointment, not panic.

"It ended when you coordinated a fatal collision and framed the one innocent man you were supposed to be rehabilitating," Stormy retorted, walking toward him, stopping near a heavy concrete barrier. "You used my father's death to recruit assets for your laundering ring. You used the VSO as a pipeline. That's why Ethan was out so quickly."

Harrison sighed, a theatrical expression of fatigue. "Recruitment is an ugly word. I prefer *asset integration.* Ethan was a perfect candidate. Intelligent, excellent work ethic, zero outside connections, and crippled by guilt. He would have been compliant and untraceable. You, Stormy, were an unexpected complication." He opened his case, revealing wads of cash. "Give me the journal. I can make your family's loss a little less painful. Say, a half million? You can take your fiancé, start that life in the Rockies."

"You killed my father, Mr. Harrison. You targeted Elias after he copied your network codes onto a microchip. Then you used Ethan's truck as the bullet," Stormy accused, holding the journal tighter. "That's murder." Harrison's façade finally cracked. His face twisted with rage. "Elias was interfering! He found out I was using his antique shop to move capital! And you—you pathetic, grieving girl—you thought you could save my best asset? You couldn't save anyone, Stormy. You just complicated a clean operation."

He took a menacing step closer. "You think I didn't see you two? That little love story in my intake room? It was pathetic. I used that idiot Mark to expose you because I knew the shame would send Ethan running. It almost worked." "It would have worked," Ethan's voice cut through the darkness. He emerged from behind the car, stepping into the dim light of the overhead lamp, his presence solid and uncompromising. "If she hadn't found the chip."

Harrison froze, his eyes darting between them. He realized the journal was the least of his problems. They had the motive and the witness.

"Vance. You should have stayed in the mountains," Harrison snarled, reaching into his jacket.

Ethan lunged forward, grabbing Harrison's wrist before he could pull a weapon. The confrontation was brutal and quick. Ethan, fueled by years of repressed guilt and the righteous fury of being framed, was terrifyingly efficient. He slammed Harrison against the concrete barrier, pinning his arm. The small, high-caliber handgun Harrison was reaching for clattered onto the pavement.

"I served five years for your cover-up," Ethan growled, his face inches from Harrison's.

"Now you serve for murder."

As if on cue, a sudden chorus of sirens wailed in the distance. Stormy had already pressed the button on the small device Peterson had given her—a simple location tracker. Peterson had moved from the café to the edge of the lot, recording the entire exchange.

Within minutes, the parking lot was swarming with police. Harrison was wrestled into cuffs, screaming about corruption and interference, but his confession captured by Peterson's discreet recording was undeniable.

The next morning, Stormy and Ethan sat in their small, empty apartment, the sunlight streaming in. The apartment was ready to be surrendered, but they were not broken. Ethan held Stormy's hand, rubbing the smooth, warm wood of her engagement ring. The truth had not shattered them; it had annealed them. "I still have to answer for my crime, Stormy," Ethan said quietly. "I drove drunk. I took a life. The murder conviction is lifted, but the manslaughter remains." "And you'll serve it with integrity," Stormy replied, leaning her head on his shoulder. "But you won't serve it alone. We cleared your name, Ethan.

You are a good man who made a terrible mistake and was used by evil. That's the truth we build on." "And you?" he asked, looking down at her. "The lies?" Stormy smiled, a genuine, peaceful smile, free of the shadow of Elias and the VSO office. "I stood in the light, Ethan. I confessed, I sought truth, and I risked everything for you. My penance is over. I earned my redemption, too." He brought her hand to his lips, kissing the wooden ring. "Then there's only one thing left to do."

Three months later, Stormy and Ethan stood on a mountain overlooking the valley near the forestry camp. Ethan, now legally cleared of the murder charges, was serving the remainder of his manslaughter sentence through community service and vocational training at the remote facility, a path he embraced with renewed humility.

They were getting married next week, a quiet ceremony attended only by Mr. Peterson and a few trusted friends. Ethan reached into his pocket and pulled out a small, heavy object. It was Elias's silver compass keychain, meticulously repaired. "The locksmith fixed the rattling," Ethan murmured, turning it over. "But Elias used to say that it kept him 'going true north.' I think it means following your internal moral compass, no matter how hard the path." He handed it to Stormy. She pressed the compass to her heart. They had both strayed from the light, but by seeking the painful truth, they had found their way back to a path of honesty. Their love was no longer a secret built on grief, but a shared journey forged in danger and cemented by truth. Their second chance was earned, not given.

The End

VI

En Espanol

Forty

Capítulo 1

El eco hueco

El silencio en el apartamento era el peor tipo de recuerdo. Era el eco de **Elias**, el padre de Stormy—un hombre cuya vida había sido ruidosa, llena de malos discos de jazz y bromas aún peores. Ahora, cuatro meses después del funeral, el silencio era absoluto y se sentía como una pesada colcha sobre todo.

Stormy se sentó en el sofá mientras la luz del sol de la tarde no calentaba la taza de porcelana astillada que tenía en las manos. Tenía veintidós años, recién graduada y de repente a la deriva. Su padre no le había dejado una gran herencia, pero sí un pequeño apartamento con alquiler controlado sobre la librería de antigüedades que él había gestionado, y un montón de preguntas sin respuesta sobre el accidente de coche que le había llevado.

La policía lo había calificado de fatalidad por conducción temeraria , donde un conductor ebrio desvió y chocó de frente contra el coche de Elias . El conductor había sobrevivido, por poco, y ahora cumplía condena en el centro penitenciario de baja seguridad justo fuera de los límites de la ciudad. Stormy había intentado leer los informes policiales, pero la jerga legal se confundía en un ruido incomprensible. Solo sabía el nombre: **Ethan Vance**.

Hace una semana, desesperada por reemplazar el vacío en el pecho por algo con propósito, Stormy había aceptado un trabajo a tiempo parcial como empleada en la oficina local de Servicios a Víctimas (VSO). Sabía que era una ironía macabra. Ella misma era una víctima, pero ahora ayudaba a otros a navegar por los sistemas que la habían fallado.

Su primera misión, que tanto temía como extrañamente anhelaba, era mañana. Era un turno de admisión en el Anexo Correccional de Riverbend. El Anexo era menos una prisión y más una fortaleza burocrática, todo bloques grises de hormigón y alambre de púas que de alguna manera aún parecían desvaídos bajo las débiles luces fluorescentes. Stormy apretó su gastado bolso de cuero marrón y la placa de vinilo VSO pegada a su blusa.

El guardia en el mostrador era un hombre llamado Gaven, con un bigote que parecía una mueca permanente y que estaba marcado por su identificación hasta que empezó a inquietarse. "Vance", murmuró, devolviéndole la identificación. "Hoy haces la admisión de Vance." Stormy se quedó paralizada. "¿Ethan Vance?"

"Sí. Evaluación de elegibilidad para la libertad condicional. Gran reunión. Solo estás registrando su documentación de perfil, nada pesado. No te preocupes, señora, el Anexo es de baja seguridad; estos tipos solo cumplen su condena." Gaven le hizo un gesto para que pasara por la puerta interior. "Pasillo C, tercera puerta a la izquierda."

El corazón de Stormy latía frenéticamente contra sus costillas. Había leído ese nombre en papeles durante meses, pero estar físicamente en el mismo edificio que el hombre que mató a su padre era como estar en una nube tóxica. Casi se dio la vuelta, pero el recuerdo de la silla vacía de su padre en la mesa de la cocina la impulsó hacia adelante. *Solo necesito verlo,* pensó, *ver al monstruo que hizo esto.* El pasillo C era estéril y resonaba. Encontró la sala de ingreso, un pequeño espacio dominado por una pesada mesa metálica. Una pila de expedientes la esperaba ordenadamente. Había llegado temprano.

Abrió el primer expediente, y allí estaba: **Ethan Vance**. Una foto policial—afeitado, ojos intensos con una leve curvatura, casi tímida, en la comisura de la boca. Parecía más joven de lo que ella esperaba, quizá veinticinco años, y absolutamente sin importancia. No era un monstruo en absoluto, solo una persona que tomó una decisión y destruyó una vida.

Una pesada puerta se deslizó detrás de ella. Dio un salto, cerrando rápidamente el expediente. "Perdona", dijo una voz profunda. "No quería asustarte. Debes ser la nueva empleada del VSO." Stormy se giró. El hombre que estaba en el umbral era más alto de lo que había imaginado por la foto policial, de complexión delgada y vestía el uniforme gris estándar. Era Ethan Vance.

Sus ojos, tan intensos, los ojos callados de la foto se centraron en ella. Llevaban un peso crudo de tristeza que contradecía instantáneamente la idea de un conductor descuidado y borracho.

"Sí", logró decir Stormy, su voz apenas un susurro. "Soy Stormy." Omitió intencionadamente su apellido, sintiendo una extraña necesidad de mantener ese secreto bajo llave.

Ethan asintió lenta y medidamente. "Es bueno por fin poner cara al servicio. Me dijeron que venía alguien nuevo." Se detuvo, bajando la mirada respetuosamente. "Gracias por estar aquí." La simple cortesía era desorientadora. Stormy esperaba desafío, arrogancia o remordimiento, pero no esta gratitud silenciosa. Caminó hacia el lado opuesto de la mesa metálica y se sentó, sus movimientos ensayados y lentos, como si cada articulación llevara una pesada carga.

"Necesito verificar información básica para su valoración, señor Vance", dijo Stormy, encontrando fuerza en la formalidad de su papel de VSO. Abrió su carpeta de nuevo, evitando los detalles del crimen. "¿Fecha de nacimiento?" Respondió él con claridad. Mientras registraba los datos, el silencio en la sala se alargó y dejó de ser la prisión y se volvió más sobre las dos personas que la habitaban.

"¿Stormy es tu nombre completo?" preguntó Ethan en voz baja, interrumpiendo su trabajo.

Stormy levantó la vista, sorprendida por la pregunta personal. "Sí. Mi padre siempre decía que nací durante una tormenta terrible." Un pequeño dolor agudo le atravesó el pecho al mencionar a Elias. Ethan escuchó, no con lástima, sino con un interés profundo y concentrado que la hizo sentirse vista por primera vez desde que murió su padre.

"Te queda bien", dijo. "Suena fuerte."

Su observación inesperada fue una grieta en el frío muro que ella había construido alrededor de su duelo. Se dio cuenta, con un sobresalto nauseabundo, de que había olvidado por completo que él era la razón por la que estaba de luto. Había olvidado, por un instante, que él era el asesino.

"Vamos a ceñirnos a la forma, señor Vance", afirmó, recuperando su tono profesional, aunque su mano temblaba ligeramente sobre el bolígrafo.

Pero la semilla estaba plantada. Stormy había venido a ver a un monstruo y en su lugar encontró a un hombre que escuchaba y que veía fuerza en su nombre.

Forty-One

Capítulo 2

El Proyecto

Stormy regresó al Anexo de Riverbend dos días después, armada con una carpeta nueva y una misión autoimpuesta por ella. Había pasado las horas intermedias investigando estadísticas de rehabilitación, leyendo artículos sobre la reincidencia y convenciéndose de que su padre, Elias, habría querido que ayudara a otros a encontrar un camino mejor. Esto no iba sobre Ethan Vance, el asesino; esto iba de Stormy, la trabajadora empática del VSO, haciendo su trabajo.

No volvió a usar la excusa de la evaluación de libertad condicional de Ethan. En su lugar, inventó un nuevo programa en curso diseñado para internos de larga duración que mostraran un remordimiento significativo y potencial para una reintegración exitosa. Su supervisor, abrumada y confiada, simplemente firmó la nueva documentación. Cuando volvió a entrar en la sala de admisión estéril, Ethan ya la esperaba. Se levantó inmediatamente cuando entró, un gesto de respeto que encontró tanto formal como encantador. "Stormy", dijo, el sonido de su nombre saliendo de su boca con una familiaridad suave que la sorprendió. "No estaba seguro de que volvieras tan pronto." "Esto forma parte del nuevo programa 'Brújula de Reintegración'", explicó, alisando una arruga inexistente en su falda. Mantuvo un tono rígido y profesional. "Implica evaluaciones individuales regulares. Tenemos que centrarnos en tus mecanismos de afrontamiento y objetivos futuros, señor Vance." Él asintió seriamente, tomando asiento. "Lo entiendo. Y por favor, solo Ethan." "Ethan", concedió, la barrera entre ellos bajando un poco más.

Las sesiones comenzaron estructuradas, basándose estrictamente en las hojas de trabajo de la VSO: *¿Cuáles son tres grandes arrepentimientos? ¿Cómo afrontas el aislamiento? Describe tu responsabilidad por el evento que llevó a tu encarcelamiento.* Las respuestas de Ethan fueron contundentes e inquebrantables. Nunca minimizó el accidente. Habló de aquella noche mencionando unas copas de más en un bar solitario, la decisión de conducir, el repentino destello de luz y el silencio aterrador que siguió con una claridad aplastante que sonaba a tormento genuino.

"It's not just the time I'm serving in here," he confessed during their third session, his eyes fixed on the tabletop. "It's the time that I've robbed from someone else. I took a life. That's the sentence I have to live with." Stormy had prepared herself for this. She had rehearsed a clinical response about cognitive restructuring. Instead, she found herself leaning forward, driven by a raw empathy she hadn't known she possessed. "¿Sabes algo del hombre al que... el hombre al que golpeaste?" preguntó, con la voz apenas audible. Ethan suspiró; un peso pesado se levantó de su pecho. "Sé que se llamaba Elías y que era padre. Los informes policiales eran claros. Rezo por su familia todos los días, Stormy. Sé que es una penitencia barata, pero es todo lo que tengo."

Su dolor genuino y palpable era un contrapunto confuso a la imagen que tenía del conductor imprudente. Stormy sintió una mezcla mareante de alivio y culpa. Sintió alivio de que no fuera un monstruo y culpa de que ocultara su identidad mientras cosechaba su dolor. "Tenemos que centrarnos en tu vida después de la liberación", Stormy los guió hacia atrás, intentando tomar el control. "¿Qué habilidades puedes desarrollar aquí? ¿Cuál es el objetivo?" "Una segunda oportunidad", dijo Ethan simplemente, mirándola. "Ser un hombre digno de esa oportunidad. Si alguna vez salgo, quiero trabajar con mis manos. Carpintería. Algo real. Algo que construya en lugar de destruya."

Durante las semanas siguientes, las sesiones de VSO fueron evolucionando. Las hojas oficiales se completaron rápidamente y el resto del tiempo se llenó de conversaciones. Stormy descubrió que Ethan era autodidacta, devorándose todos los libros que tenía la biblioteca de la prisión. Era perspicaz, irónicamente humorístico y ferozmente protector con los internos más débiles. Se encontró compartiendo detalles de su propia vida: sus luchas tras la muerte de su padre, su amor por las películas antiguas y su frustración con su vida posgraduada sin rumbo.

Nunca mencionaba a Elias por su nombre, refiriéndose solo a "la pérdida". Ethan, percibiendo la profundidad de su dolor, le ofreció un consuelo silencioso. "Perder a un padre cambia el eje de tu mundo", dijo una vez, compartiendo una historia sobre la lejana muerte de su propia madre. "Está bien sentirse perdido. El silencio que dejan atrás es ensordecedor." Entendía el silencio y su dolor. No sabía que él era la causa, pero también era la única persona que parecía validarlo de verdad. La ironía era un nudo en su estómago, pero la recompensa emocional de su atención era demasiado adictiva para rendirse.

Una tarde, mientras recogía sus materiales, Ethan la detuvo. "Stormy, sé que esto es muy inapropiado y respeto los límites de tu trabajo, pero… verte cada semana, es lo único que se siente real aquí. Me das esperanza." Stormy miró su rostro sincero, viendo más allá del uniforme gris al hombre que se estaba convirtiendo en la persona más importante de su vida solitaria. Sus dedos se movieron. Quería acercarse, tranquilizarle.

Le estoy ayudando a reformarse, racionalizó, reprimiendo el pánico creciente por su secreto. *Es un buen hombre que cometió un terrible error. Se merece una segunda oportunidad.* "Sigue trabajando en tus habilidades de carpintería, Ethan", dijo, con voz más suave de lo que pretendía. "Sigue leyendo. Es la mejor esperanza que tienes."

La puerta se deslizó y el guardia le dio la señal universal de que *el tiempo se fuera*. Al salir, el nudo del engaño se apretó. Esto ya no era solo un proyecto de VSO; era una relación construida sobre una base de arena movediza.

Forty-Two

Capítulo 3

El desbloqueo

La noticia no llegó en el silencio aséptico de la sala del VSO, sino a través de una llamada telefónica impactante e inesperada de su supervisor, el señor Harrison.

"Stormy, ¿estás sentada? Vance. Ethan Vance. Va a ser el ejemplo perfecto de tu programa Reintegration Compass." Stormy, que rellenaba informes de gastos en la silenciosa oficina del VSO, apretó el auricular tan fuerte que se le pusieron blancos los nudillos. "¿Qué pasa con él, señor Harrison?"

"La junta revisó su caso, tus informes completos y su historial impecable de conducta. Aceleraron su audiencia de libertad condicional. Fue esta mañana. Está fuera. Libertad condicional, permiso laboral, todo el paquete. Con efecto el próximo viernes." La voz del señor Harrison era alegre, ajena al pánico que le apoderaba el pecho a Stormy. "¡Un milagro, Stormy! ¡Has conseguido un milagro!"

Consiguió decir ahogado, "Eso es… una noticia maravillosa," antes de colgar, su mente era un mareo de incredulidad y terror.

Ethan. ¿Libre?

En el entorno controlado del Anexo, ella era la guardiana, la que poseía el poder del conocimiento—su conocimiento de su crimen, su identidad secreta. Fuera, en el mundo real, serían dos personas como iguales, con una conexión profunda construida sobre su mentira intencionada. La mentira de repente se sintió enorme, asfixiante.

Tenía exactamente una semana para decidir. Si cortaba el contacto ahora, podría racionalizarlo como que mantenía límites profesionales. Podía fingir que la intensidad de su conexión era solo un efecto secundario del trabajo de alta presión de VSO. Pero la idea de no volver a verle jamás, de dejar que el silencio y el dolor volvieran, le provocó una punzada fría de soledad.

Stormy fue al Anexo esa misma noche, programando una entrevista de salida de emergencia. Gaven, el guardia, sonrió levemente. "Está listo para ti, hacedor de milagros." Ethan paseaba por la pequeña habitación, con los ojos brillando con una mezcla de asombro y miedo. Cuando la vio, se detuvo, pareciendo un hombre que de repente había olvidado cómo respirar el aire libre.

"Stormy", susurró, caminando rápidamente hacia la mesa. "No sé qué decir. Es por tu culpa. Tus informes… tu guía… me hiciste creer que había algo externo por lo que valía la pena trabajar." "Fue tu esfuerzo, Ethan", insistió, dejando el maletín sobre el suelo. Podía sentir cómo las paredes de su personalidad profesional se desmoronaban.

"No." Negó con la cabeza con sinceridad que irradiaba. "Antes de ti, solo contaba minutos. Ahora… Cuento los días hasta poder demostrarte a ti y a mí mismo que puedo ser el hombre que creísteis que podía ser. El que construye en lugar de destruir." Su uso de la palabra "construye" reflejaba su conversación anterior. Había tomado su aliento abstracto y lo había forjado en un futuro tangible y esperanzador. Sintió una oleada abrumadora de orgullo y afecto, que momentáneamente eclipsó el secreto mortal entre ellos.

Ella le miró, realmente le miró y la intensa tristeza en sus ojos, la ligera forma en que sujetaba las manos como si aún esperara que las esposas terminaran y que el debate interno terminara. Su padre se había ido. Ethan estaba allí. Se había reformado, cambiado y la amaba. No podía soltarla. No ahora. "Ethan", empezó, con la voz baja y temblorosa. "Yo... Conozco los protocolos. No debería. Pero no puedo dejar de verte. No ahora. No cuando por fin has salido." Su rostro se iluminó con una sonrisa vacilante pero llena de alegría que borraba años de desesperación institucional. "Stormy, no me atreví a preguntar. Conozco las reglas. Pero te necesito. De verdad."

"Necesitarás un lugar donde trabajar, un trabajo al que rendir cuentas", dijo, volviendo rápidamente a la logística para mantener el control. "Conozco un lugar. El dueño de la librería de antigüedades bajo mi edificio de apartamentos busca ayuda con restauraciones y estructuras. Carpintería ligera. Es un viejo amigo de mi familia."

Este fue su primer gran paso al otro lado de la línea: organizar su trabajo a pocos metros de su casa. Era arriesgado, pero le daba una forma de verlo constantemente sin cruzar formalmente la línea del VSO. "¿Lo haces por mí?" preguntó Ethan, con la voz cargada de emoción. "Hago esto porque mereces una segunda oportunidad, Ethan", repitió, aferrándose desesperadamente a la narrativa reformista.

El viernes siguiente también parecía un día de lanzamiento para Stormy. Esperó en su apartamento, observando desde la ventana cómo una maltrevida furgoneta VSO dejaba a Ethan cerca de la librería de antigüedades. Parecía incómodo con ropa prestada; vaqueros y un jersey gris claro pero completamente transformado. Se instaló en la pequeña habitación subvencionada organizada por el dueño de la librería, el señor Peterson, un hombre generoso y algo excéntrico que adoraba a Elias. Stormy pasó los días siguientes vigilando su progreso con una ansiedad meticulosa. Ethan cumplió su palabra mientras trabajaba largas y arduas horas, dedicándose a lijar, teñir y reparar delicadas las estructuras.

Su relación fuera de la prisión se sentía como navegar por un paisaje hermoso y frágil. Su primera cita oficial fue una tranquila noche en la azotea del edificio de su apartamento, con vistas al resplandeciente paisaje urbano. "Mira eso", murmuró Ethan, con la voz cargada de asombro. "No he visto estrellas así en cinco años."

Stormy se sentó a su lado, sus hombros apenas se tocaban. "Son las mismas estrellas, Ethan. Ahora solo tienes la libertad de mirar hacia arriba." Él tomó su mano, la palma áspera y callosa por el trabajo. Su toque envió una corriente de calor a través de ella, una calidez que finalmente empezó a derretir la fría cáscara del dolor que había vivido desde la muerte de su padre. Ella apretó su mano de vuelta, reconociendo el compromiso emocional que ambos habían asumido. Fue en esos momentos de desconfianza cuando la relación se profundizó rápidamente. Stormy vio al hombre amable y reflexivo en que se había convertido. Ethan vio a la mujer compasiva bajo la armadura profesional.

Un mes después, cuando la besó por primera vez, fue un encuentro tierno y vacilante de labios que albergaba años de anhelo contenido. Stormy finalmente se permitió creer que no había sido un error terrible. Esto era real. Era la única persona que entendía su soledad, aunque él fuera la razón. Sin embargo, la mentira se fue pudriendo. La habían presentado al señor Peterson como "Stormy Lee." Ethan la conocía como Stormy. Pero la dueña de la librería a veces se deslizaba. Un martes lluvioso, el señor Peterson le mostraba a Ethan un complicado proyecto de restauración. "Esto pertenecía a Elias, el padre de Stormy. Pobre hombre, se lo llevaron demasiado pronto." Ethan se quedó paralizado, abriendo los ojos de par en par. Miró a Stormy, que estaba cerca, colocando una estantería. "¿Elias? ¿El nombre de tu padre era Elias?" El estómago de Stormy se hundió. Ese era el momento. Tenía que afrontarlo, o todo el engaño se desmoronaría en ese momento.

"Sí", dijo, acercándose a la voz, manteniendo la voz firme a pesar del cambio sísmico que se producía bajo ella. "Elias Thompson. ¿Por qué? ¿Reconoces el nombre, Ethan?" Ethan relajó los hombros, con el ceño ligeramente fruncido. "No, no. Es solo que... es un nombre bonito. Pensé que lo habías mencionado antes, quizá." Esbozó una pequeña sonrisa cálida.

"Mis disculpas. He estado tan concentrado en acertar con estas piezas." Lo había descartado. No relacionó a "Elias Thompson", la víctima de su crimen, con "Elias", el padre de la mujer a la que amaba. Los periódicos y los informes se centraban en el crimen, las fechas, la dirección, no la vida. Seguía centrado en su propio remordimiento, no en la biografía de la víctima. Stormy sintió una oleada de alivio mareante, seguida al instante por una vergüenza profunda. Había escapado de la verdad de nuevo. Pero sabía, en el fondo, que su suerte no duraría para siempre.

Forty-Three

Capítulo 4

Construyendo una vida

Los seis meses siguientes fueron los más felices que Stormy había conocido. El apartamento, que antes era tumba de la memoria de Elias y del aislamiento de Stormy, se convirtió en un hogar rebosante de energía compartida. Ethan se mudó oficialmente dos meses después de su liberación. Llevaba poco consigo—un puñado de libros, una Biblia de cuero gastada—pero su presencia llenaba el espacio por completo.

Era meticulosamente ordenado, casi obsesivamente, un efecto persistente de la vida en prisión. Nunca alzaba la voz. Trataba a Stormy con una reverencia silenciosa, como si fuera lo más frágil y valioso que había conocido. Su amor no era salvaje ni tumultuoso; era una corriente constante de devoción. Los viernes por la noche, tras el cierre de la librería del señor Peterson, Ethan recogía la pequeña mesa de la cocina y enseñaba a Stormy lo básico de la ebanistería, demostrando cómo encajar piezas de madera sin problemas, encerrándolas en un vínculo irrompible. "Eso es lo que estamos haciendo, Stormy", decía, lijando los bordes ásperos de una pequeña caja de joyas que estaba haciendo para ella. "Estamos tomando todas estas piezas toscas como mi pasado, tu dolor y encontrando los ángulos precisos donde encajan. Estamos creando algo nuevo y sólido."

La rehabilitación de Ethan fue genuina. Se ofreció voluntario para reparar casas para ancianos del barrio. Sus manos, antes acostumbradas a conducir sin cuidado, ahora dedicadas a arreglar y construir. Escribió cartas de disculpa al juez y al oficial de libertad condicional, expresando su profundo agradecimiento por su segunda oportunidad. Stormy lo observaba, su corazón hinchándose con una emoción que era parte amor, parte orgullo y parte profunda y nauseabunda culpa. Él era el hombre que ella había ayudado a crear, el alma reformada por la que había luchado. ¿Cómo podía esta persona dulce y devota ser el mismo hombre que destrozó su mundo?

La verdad del crimen se convirtió en un fantasma. A la luz del día de su vida juntos, parecía imposible que Ethan fuera la misma persona que aparecía en el frío expediente policial. Había logrado compartimentar: estaba Ethan Vance, el carpintero amable y cariñoso, y estaba Ethan Vance, el delincuente encarcelado. Se negaba a dejar que ambos se solapasen. Sus citas eran sencillas: picnics junto al lago de la ciudad, curiosear por secciones olvidadas de la biblioteca pública y largas conversaciones sobre libros y filosofía. Stormy se sorprendió riendo con facilidad, de verdad, por primera vez desde la muerte de su padre. Ethan le había devuelto su eje a su vida.

Cuando discutían, siempre era algo menor, normalmente por su insistencia en asumir la responsabilidad de cada tarea, nacida del miedo a fallarla o a perder la vida que habían construido. Una noche, hablaban de futuros viajes, y Stormy mencionó casualmente hacer un viaje por carretera por la Costa Oeste. El rostro de Ethan se nubló de inmediato.

"No", dijo, con voz plana. "No creo que pueda hacer eso, Stormy." "¿Por qué no?" Apretó con fuerza su vaso de agua. "No voy a conducir largas distancias. No puedo. Nunca me pondré en una posición en la que pueda repetir ese error. Aunque esté sobrio, aunque tenga cuidado. Simplemente no lo haré."

Era un recordatorio doloroso y contundente. Su incapacidad para conducir era una manifestación física de su inmensa y constante culpa por el accidente que mató a su padre. En lugar de alejarla, su miedo consolidó su creencia en su reforma. Se castigaba a diario; realmente era un hombre diferente.

"Vale", dijo Stormy con suavidad, poniendo su mano sobre la suya, "entonces iremos en tren. O yo conduzco. Lo resolveremos. La cuestión es estar juntos." El compromiso se profundizó de forma natural. Navegaron las fiestas juntos. Compartieron una Navidad tranquila y conmovedora, marcada por la consideración de Ethan al crear pequeños regalos tallados a mano. Conocieron a los pocos amigos universitarios que quedaban de Stormy, que, aunque al principio escépticos con la historia del 'exconvicto', pronto se dejaron conquistar por la actitud humilde y atenta de Ethan.

Una ventosa mañana de sábado a principios de primavera, Ethan insistió en subir hasta la cima del mirador del embalse de la ciudad cercano. Hacía frío, pero la vista de su pequeña ciudad extendida bajo ellos era impresionante. Ethan estaba inusualmente callado en la ascensión. Cuando llegaron a la cima, la condujo a una pequeña repisa privada protegida por pinos. No se arrodilló de forma cinematográfica; en cambio, se quedó frente a ella, con sus intensos ojos fijos en los de ella. De su bolsillo sacó una pequeña caja forrada de terciopelo. Dentro había un anillo que él mismo había confeccionado. Era una simple alianza de plata incrustada con un trozo de madera oscura y recuperada, pulida hasta brillar como un espejo.

"Esta madera", dijo, sosteniéndola con cuidado, "está rescatada de un antiguo banco de iglesia. Ha visto mucho fracaso, mucha gracia y mucha esperanza silenciosa y persistente." Su voz estaba áspera por la emoción. "Stormy, me salvaste la vida. Me reconstruiste. Me diste más que una segunda oportunidad; me diste una razón para ser digno de ella. Sé que mi pasado es oscuro, pero mi futuro solo es brillante si tú estás en él. Cásate conmigo."

Las lágrimas corrían por las mejillas de Stormy. Eran lágrimas de alegría, y lágrimas de una profunda y terrible culpa. Miró al hombre sincero y maravilloso que tenía delante, un hombre que había admitido su crimen y trabajaba incansablemente para redimirse, que la amaba sinpensar. Ignoró la voz del recuerdo de su padre susurrando en el fondo de su mente.

"Sí", se atragantó. "Sí, Ethan, me casaré contigo." Le deslizó el anillo en el dedo y, por un momento, el ajuste le pareció increíblemente perfecto. La envolvió en un abrazo tan fuerte que casi le partió las costillas, una manifestación física de su miedo y amor. Mientras bajaban la montaña cogidas de la mano, Stormy sintió una alegría emocionante e imprudente. Estaba prometida con el hombre más increíble que había conocido jamás. La boda estaba prevista para dentro de seis meses—una hermosa ceremonia otoñal. La planificación de la boda comenzó de inmediato, consumiendo todo su tiempo libre y reforzando su compromiso. Eran un equipo, planificando su futuro, consolidando la mentira más profundamente en los cimientos de su vida.

Mientras Stormy y Ethan van de compras para el vestido de novia, se encuentran con Mark, un antiguo compañero de Elias, que reconoce el rostro de Ethan Vance por los informes de accidentes de alto perfil. Mark revela públicamente a Ethan que Stormy es hija de Elias Thompson. La revelación destroza a Ethan, que ve su amor como un acto calculado de control y venganza. La rechaza y huye de la ciudad, buscando una penitencia honesta y solitaria.

Ethan se retira al taller de la librería. Stormy confiesa todo su engaño al señor Peterson, quienofrece consejo pero confirma sus temores de haber comprometido la verdadera redención de Ethan . Ethan le devuelve el anillo a Stormy, negándose a reconciliarse, diciendo que no puede vivir una vida basada en una mentira y que debe ganarse su verdad solo. Se va a trabajar en la silvicultura en las Rocosas.

Forty-Four

Capítulo 5

El peso de la memoria

Stormy era un recipiente vacío de sonido y propósito. Se sentó en medio del suelo del salón, la luz del sol filtrándose por las cortinas iluminando las motas de polvo que danzaban en el aire—las mismas motas de polvo que ella y Ethan solían ver juntos. Ahora, el apartamento era un museo de su fracaso.

Cogió un himnario gastado encuadernado en cuero de la mesa de centro, un vestigio de su infancia. Las páginas eran finas, marcadas con la elegante caligrafía de su madre y pasajes subrayados. El recuerdo de su padre, Elias, padre soltero, y el profundo papel de la iglesia en sus vidas, la invadió.

Su madre, María, había sido una mujer dulce y luminosa cuya vida había sido un testimonio de fe y devoción. Murió al dar a luz a Stormy. La tragedia no fue una enfermedad persistente, sino una pérdida repentina y violenta que marcó el inicio de la vida de Stormy con un vacío inmediato y profundo. Elias nunca se volvió a casar. Se dedicó por completo a criar a su hija como un memorial vivo para su esposa.

"Tu madre me dio la mayor tormenta y la mayor luz", solía decirle Elías, tocándole la mejilla con su áspera mano de carpintero. A menudo estaba callado, atormentado por la ausencia de su esposa, pero volcó todo su amor en Tormenta.

Su vida estaba anclada en la iglesia. Era una pequeña parroquia histórica en el centro donde María había servido como profesora de escuela dominical. Para Elías, la fe no era una elección; era una fuerza sostenida. Él y María habían inculcado en Stormy una brújula moral feroz: una arraigada en la honestidad absoluta, la penitencia por los errores y la creencia inquebrantable de que la verdad, por dolorosa que fuera, era el camino hacia la gracia de Dios.

"Somos gente Thompson", decía Elias, refiriéndose a su apellido, que ella había ocultado a Ethan. "Y la gente Thompson no trata en sombras, Stormy. Nos mantenemos en la luz, incluso cuando arde."

Esta historia profunda y compartida era la fuente del dolor más profundo de Stormy y de su conflicto moral más agonizante. Elias no era solo un padre; era su mundo entero, el único guardián de su identidad y el guardián de la memoria de su madre. Cuando murió, el eje de su mundo no solo cambió, sino que desapareció. La pérdida de Elias no solo le había quitado un padre; había tomado a su compañero de fe, la única persona que realmente comprendía la profundidad de su legado. Su dolor, por tanto, no era solo tristeza; era una soledad desesperada y existencial.

La realización que la golpeaba ahora, sentada en las ruinas de su relación con Ethan, era la profundidad de su traición moral. Al perseguir a Ethan, no solo le había mentido; había mentido a la memoria de su madre, había traicionado las enseñanzas de su padre y profanado los principios de honestidad que su fe exigía.

Su relación con Ethan, el hombre que ahora intentaba encontrar su propio camino honesto en las montañas, era la sombra más profunda que jamás había proyectado. Le había animado a buscar la redención mientras ella misma nadaba en un mar de engaños.

Él quitó una vida, pensó, presionando el himnario contra su pecho. *Y yo le quité su verdad.* El dolor de Ethan se amplificó porque comprendió el verdadero peso del pecado y la redención, un peso como la base espiritual sobre la que ella había crecido. Él había buscado la gracia a través de la honestidad y el trabajo duro; ella le había ofrecido un respiro construido sobre un terrible y frágil secreto. Si Elias hubiera estado vivo, habría exigido justicia y honestidad. Si María hubiera estado viva, habría ofrecido perdón, pero solo mediante confesión. Stormy no ofreció ninguno de los dos. Simplemente enterró la verdad bajo el peso de su amor.

El peso de la lucha solitaria de su padre por criarla, su devoción a la memoria de su madre y su repentino y violento final se condensaron en una presión abrumadora. No solo necesitaba a Ethan; necesitaba que validara su vida, que llenara el vacío que dejó la pérdida de las únicas dos personas que realmente la habían amado.

La base moral, antes tan sólida, se desmoronaba bajo sus pies. Stormy se dio cuenta de que la elección no era solo entre **el Amor o la Justicia**; era entre **el Amor o la Verdad**. Había elegido un amor construido sobre una mentira, y ahora había perdido ambos.

Fue esta desesperación, ese profundo sentido de fracasar con su propio legado moral, lo que le dio la energía temeraria para buscar respuestas donde antes no lo había hecho. Si no podía tener a Ethan, al menos podría restaurar la integridad de su padre y, quizás, encontrar un camino hacia su propio perdón. Impulsada por una necesidad desesperada de mantenerse al margen de la luz, apartó el himnario y caminó hacia la pequeña caja cerrada donde guardaba sus pertenencias más dolorosas y protegidas: los informes originales de la policía sobre el accidente fatal de Elias Thompson.

Forty-Five

Capítulo 6

El detalle oculto

Stormy abrió la caja. Los informes policiales, las declaraciones de los testigos y el expediente de homicidio vehicular estaban exactamente como los había dejado. Los consideraba rígidos, fríos e impersonales. Siempre había evitado leer los detalles demasiado de cerca, prefiriendo el horror abstracto del crimen a los dolorosos detalles.

Ahora, leía cada línea, impulsada por un deseo perverso de encontrar algo, cualquier cosa, que pudiera aliviar la culpa de Ethan o, egoístamente, justificar su mentira.

Los informes detallaban el accidente: Elias Thompson conducía su sedán en dirección este por la Ruta 17 tras una noche tardía gestionando la librería. Ethan Vance conducía su pickup en dirección oeste, cruzando la línea central tras consumir una gran cantidad de alcohol. Colisión frontal. Sin ambigüedades.

Sin embargo, mientras leía, un detalle, previamente pasado por alto en su dolor y prisa, había captado su atención: una nota marginal en el informe del reconstruccionista de tráfico. Se refería a un testigo secundario, un conductor anónimo que había seguido el coche de Elias Thompson durante varios kilómetros justo antes del accidente.

El testigo afirmó que el sedán del señor Thompson había estado "conduciendo de forma errática" y se había desviado brevemente hacia el carril de avería antes de corregirse bruscamente, momentos antes de la colisión. La policía desestimó la observación, atribuyendo el movimiento de Elias a la típica fatiga nocturna, especialmente dado el indiscutible estado de embriaguez de Ethan Vance.

Pero Stormy conocía a su padre. Elias era un hombre meticuloso, casi en exceso. Nunca había sido imprudente. Sin embargo, un registro de inventario aparte llamó su atención: entre los efectos de Elias encontrados en la escena había un pequeño frasco sin abrir de analgésicos con receta en su guantera. La receta data de varios meses, dada por un brote de dolor crónico de espalda.

Los informes confirmaron que se había realizado un análisis toxicológico estándar a Elias. Nunca había preguntado por los resultados y solo se centraba en el TAC de Ethan. Revisó la última página del inventario forense hasta encontrar la sección: "Resultados toxicológicos de la víctima: negativo para alcohol. Se detectaron trazas de analgésico con receta (hidrocodona). Por debajo del umbral terapéutico."

¿Por debajo del umbral terapéutico? Significaba que no estaba afectado según la letra de la ley.

Pero un frío de temor se instaló en el estómago de Stormy. Su padre siempre se había negado a tomar esas pastillas porque le daban sueño. ¿Había tomado una esa noche tarde? ¿Había causado la medicación, junto con su fatiga, la "conducción errática" momentánea que describió el testigo? ¿Ethan Vance, borracho y a toda velocidad, había desviado hacia Elias, o Elias se había desviado brevemente en la trayectoria del camión de Ethan que venía de frente?

La colisión seguía siendo culpa de Ethan—su intoxicación fue la causa inmediata. Pero el accidente de repente parecía menos un crimen monstruoso y unilateral y más un encuentro catastrófico de dos errores: uno borracho y otro somnoliento. Si había aunque fuera un pequeño grado de culpa por parte de su padre, eso lo cambiaba todo. Significaba que Ethan Vance no había asesinado a un santo inocente. Significaba que su crimen, aunque terrible, era menos el acto de un monstruo puramente destructivo y más el trágico resultado de un fallo sistémico, uno que implicaba el propio error de juicio de su padre.

Este pequeño detalle oculto no era una absolución, pero sí una complicación crucial. Era un pequeño pinchazo de gris moral que podría ser suficiente para salvar a Ethan del peso aplastante de la culpa singular que llevaba. Era una culpa que ella había explotado.

Se dio cuenta de lo que tenía que hacer. Tenía que soportar todo el peso de su engaño y la fragilidad oculta de su padre y presentárselo a Ethan, no para recuperarlo, sino para ser finalmente honesta con él. Para confesar la verdad de su amor y la nueva, terrible verdad del accidente antes de que él desapareciera para siempre.

Forty-Six

Capítulo 7

La confrontación final

Stormy encontró a Ethan donde sabía que estaría , que era en el pequeño apartamento prestado sobre la librería, empaquetando sus pocas pertenencias. La habitación estaba casi vacía, solo con el aroma a serrín y el aire limpio y cortante de la finalidad. No levantó la vista cuando ella entró.

"Necesito cinco minutos, Ethan", dijo, con voz firme ahora, sin las súplicas que había usado antes. "Y necesito que escuches con el corazón abierto, no con el cínico que creé."

Hizo una pausa, sosteniendo una pesada copia de El Conde de Montecristo. "El corazón abierto murió en la tienda de novias, Stormy." Ignoró la puñalada. Se acercó a la pequeña mesa y extendió los archivos policiales, las notas del reconstruccionista de tráfico y el informe toxicológico.

"Esto no va de la mentira que te conté", comenzó, señalando las secciones. "Es sobre la mentira que te has estado diciendo para sobrevivir, y la que mi familia ha estado diciendo para llorar. Sé que eres culpable, Ethan. Sé que estabas borracho y que cruzaste la línea. Pero también encontré esto." Tocó los dos informes: la mención del testigo anónimo de que Elias conducía "erráticamente" y la nota sobre las cantidades mínimas de hidrocodona.

"Mi padre", continuó Stormy, su voz se rompió en una repentina oleada de dolor complicado, "era un buen hombre, pero luchaba contra el dolor y la fatiga. Tomó pastillas que no debía, y estaba desviándose justo antes del impacto. No fue solo tu error, Ethan. Fue una terrible colisión cósmica de dos personas tomando malas decisiones en un camino oscuro."

Ethan finalmente miró los papeles, el ceño fruncido, y luego a ella. Su rostro era un mapa de confusión y dolor profundo y fresco. "Estás intentando disculparme", acusó, con voz áspera. "Estás intentando echar la culpa a tu propio padre para que me retenga aquí."

"No", dijo Stormy, empujando los informes hacia él. "Te digo la verdad para que por fin puedas ser verdaderamente redimido. No tienes que cargar con todo el peso de ser el asesino de un inocente. Llevas el peso de ser imprudente. Llevas el peso de quitar una vida, sí, pero no el peso de ser un monstruo." Se levantó, cruzando las manos. "Soy la hija del hombre al que golpeaste. Y estoy perdidamente enamorada del hombre en el que te convertiste. No me importa si eres la asesina; solo me importa que seas honesta. Si te quedas, reconstruiremos. No con una mentira, sino con dos personas rotas que son responsables de sus decisiones."

Ethan recogió lentamente los informes, con las manos temblorosas mientras miraba las notas toxicológicas. La información era un pequeño y frío consuelo, y una franja gris en la absoluta oscuridad de su culpa. "No puedo quedarme, Stormy", dijo finalmente, con la voz cargada de tristeza. "Incluso con esto... Necesito ganarme mi perdón en soledad. Necesito demostrarme a mí mismo que el hombre del que te enamoraste es el hombre que puedo ser cuando nadie te vea."

La miró, su amor innegable, pero templado por una absoluta necesidad moral. "Me mentiste. Me llevé a tu padre. Ahora mismo somos veneno el uno para el otro. Esta información es para ti, Stormy. Es para tu paz con Elias. Pero no cambia lo que debo hacer." Cogió su pequeña bolsa de viaje.

"Te volveré a encontrar", prometió, con la mirada intensa. "Pero solo cuando haya reconstruido una base honesta y completa. No volveré hasta saber que merezco tu amor." Salió, dejando a Stormy sola entre los escombros de su partida y la fría y nueva realidad de la inocencia imperfecta de su padre. La verdad había salido a la luz, pero el amor se había ido, retrasado por la penitencia y la confianza rota.

Forty-Seven

Capítulo 8

La serpiente en los detalles

La ausencia de Ethan dejó una herida que Stormy ya no pudo ignorar ni intentar curar con cariño. Su periodo de penitencia fue rápido y doloroso. Renunció al trabajo de VSO, ofreciendo una explicación críptica y lo bastante honesta al señor Harrison sobre un "profundo fracaso ético" relacionado con un caso reciente. Vendió el apartamento, incapaz de soportar el silencio opresivo de un lugar que había albergado su mayor amor y su mayor engaño.

El anillo de compromiso —la alianza de madera y plata recuperada— permanecía en su dedo, ya no un símbolo de esperanza sino un pesado recordatorio de su responsabilidad. Ahora vivía sencilla, alquilando una pequeña habitación sobre una tintorería y dedicando su tiempo a investigar los últimos días de la vida de su padre.

Tenía que conocer toda la verdad del accidente, no solo la verdad parcial que le había presentado a Ethan. Releyó los archivos cientos de veces, hasta que la jerga legal se difuminó, buscando cualquier detalle que apuntara a un accidente.

Una tarde, mientras comparaba fotos de la escena del accidente, notó una anomalía. Las fotos policiales mostraban el coche de Elias—un sedán—completamente destrozado en el lado del conductor, pero un objeto estaba curiosamente conservado: el antiguo llavero plateado que siempre llevaba, junto al accidente. Contenía las llaves de su sedán y de la librería. El llavero era ornamentado, con forma de brújula antigua.

Recordaba el informe del testigo que decía que Elias había "corregido bruscamente" justo antes del impacto. ¿Por qué habría desviado? Stormy fue a ver al señor Peterson en la librería de antigüedades, buscando consuelo e información. Ahora parecía mayor, agobiado por el conocimiento del secreto de Stormy y la silenciosa marcha de Ethan . "Ha llamado, Stormy", dijo Peterson en voz baja, pasando un trapo por un escritorio restaurado. "Ethan. Trabaja para un servicio forestal cerca de las Rocosas. Está a salvo. Dijo que está pagando su deuda con trabajo honesto." "Lo sé", respondió Stormy, sacando las fotos descoloridas del accidente. "Pero la deuda no es solo con Elias, señor Peterson. Es con la verdad." Señaló la foto del llavero de brújula plateado. "¿Alguna vez notaste algo extraño en esto? Justo después del funeral, antes de coger las llaves, ¿parecía dañado?"

Peterson frunció el ceño, inclinándose más cerca. "¿La brújula? No, estaba bien. Elias la valoraba. Decía que le mantenía 'yendo hacia el norte puro', sea lo que sea que eso significara. La había arreglado solo unas semanas antes... antes del accidente."

"¿Arreglado?" preguntó Stormy, con el corazón desbocado. "¿Qué le pasaba?" Peterson pensó un momento. "Estaba traqueteando, dijo. La llevó a un reparador de la 5ª Calle, un cerrajero. Dijo que la carcasa alrededor de la aguja estaba floja. ¿Por qué?" Stormy no respondió. Conocía la naturaleza meticulosa de su padre. Si la brújula estuviera floja, la habría arreglado inmediatamente. Pero, ¿y si el "traqueteo" no era un problema de reparación, sino algo colocado dentro? Al día siguiente, localizó al cerrajero de la 5ª Calle.

El hombre, viejo y cansado, apenas recordaba la reparación. Pero cuando Stormy sacó la foto de la brújula, su memoria se aclaró.

"Ah, la brújula. Señor Thompson. Buen hombre. Pensó que la carcasa de la aguja se estaba suelta. Pero no era la carcasa." El cerrajero se inclinó, bajando la voz en tono conspirativo. "He encontrado algo dentro del hueco donde debería estar la bisagra. No era la bisagra. Era un objeto diminuto y extraño. "¿Qué tipo de objeto?" insistió Stormy, inclinándose sobre la encimera.

"Un chip", dijo el hombre, bajando aún más la voz. "Un microchip negro diminuto, como sacado de un teléfono. Lo saqué, lo metí en un sobre pequeño pegado y se lo enseñé. Puso una expresión en la cara, pálido como un fantasma. Dijo: 'Eso es. Esa es la razón.' Me pagó el doble y me dijo que olvidara haberlo visto."

Stormy sintió cómo la sangre se le iba de la cara. Un microchip. Algo que Elias consideraba lo suficientemente importante como para pagar a un cerrajero para que lo quitara discretamente, y lo bastante importante como para provocar el comentario: *"Esa es la razón." Un microchip es un dispositivo de rastreo.*

La aterradora realización la golpeó con la fuerza de la propia colisión. Elias no conducía de forma errática solo por la medicación y la fatiga. Le estaban rastreando. El testimonio de Elias "desviándose bruscamente" de repente adquirió un significado siniestro nuevo. No solo había desviado por fatiga; probablemente se había dado cuenta de que le estaban siguiendo o persiguiendo. Intentaba perder a quien le seguía. ¿Y la colisión frontal? No fue solo un conductor ebrio cometiendo un error fatal. La camioneta de Ethan Vance simplemente estaba en el lugar equivocado en el momento adecuado para alguien que quería a Elias Thompson muerto.

Stormy corrió de vuelta a su habitación alquilada, sacando de nuevo los archivos. Encontró la foto policial de la camioneta destrozada de Ethan.

La parte delantera estaba destrozada por el impacto frontal. Pero notó una pequeña y casi imperceptible marca de arañazo en el retrovisor del lado del pasajero de la camioneta de Ethan—un leve raspón que parecía sospechosamente un impacto secundario y de repaso. Un impacto que habría ocurrido momentos *antes* del choque frontal, posiblemente de otro vehículo intentando sacar a Elias de la carretera y ponerlo en el camino de Ethan. La muerte de Elias Thompson no fue un accidente. Fue un asesinato orquestado para parecer una muerte por conducir ebrio.

Y Ethan Vance, el hombre que había luchado con el peso abrumador de ser un asesino, no era más que un peón involuntario usado para completar el asesinato. No fue la causa de la muerte de Elias, sino cómplice del asesinato. Fue usado y destruido por una mano oculta. La misión de Stormy cambió al instante. No se trataba de buscar redención personal ni salvar a un hombre atormentado; se trataba de exponer una conspiración mortal, limpiar el nombre del hombre que amaba y traer verdadera justicia a la memoria de su padre. Tenía que encontrar a Ethan y decirle la verdad.

Forty-Eight

Capítulo 9

La nueva verdad

Las coordenadas proporcionadas por el señor Peterson llevaron a Stormy al interior de las Rocosas de Montana, hasta un pequeño campamento aislado gestionado por un servicio forestal sin ánimo de lucro. Era un lugar de pinos y granitos infinitos, donde el aire era frío y limpio, y el cielo parecía más cercano que el suelo. Encontró a Ethan no en la oficina del campamento, sino en un sendero a kilómetros de la civilización, vestido con ropa de trabajo utilitaria. Su rostro estaba sombreado por un sombrero de ala ancha. Estaba apoyado en un tronco enorme de árbol mientras usaba sus manos callosas trabajando un bloque de cedro tosco con un pequeño cuchillo afilado, tallando la madera en una forma intrincada y abstracta. Su penitencia, se dio cuenta, era perpetua.

Se acercó en silencio, el crujido de sus botas sobre las agujas secas de pino anunciando su presencia solo unos instantes antes de llegar a él. El cuchillo de Ethan se quedó paralizado a mitad de movimiento. Alzó la vista, y el shock en sus ojos fue instantáneo y profundo, seguido inmediatamente por el familiar y cansado resentimiento. "Stormy", dijo, con la voz ronca, áspera por la falta de uso. No se levantó, no sonrió ni movió el cuchillo. "No deberías estar aquí."

"Lo sé", respondió ella, con la respiración atrapada en la garganta, no por la caminata, sino por la intensidad cruda de verlo de nuevo. Él era más delgado, más rudo, pero la integridad de la que se había enamorado irradiaba de él como un calor físico. Todavía llevaba el anillo de madera. "He venido porque he encontrado una nueva mentira." Ethan resopló, volviendo a su talla. "Ya no tengo capacidad para mentiras, Stormy. Tuyas ni mías."

"No es nuestro", insistió, dando un paso más cerca. "Pertenece a la persona que nos tendió una trampa. Ethan, tú no fuiste la causa de la muerte de mi padre. Tú fuiste el arma." Metió la mano en su mochila y sacó el sobre manila que contenía los informes de policía, la tarjeta de visita del cerrajero y sus propias fotos anotadas. No se las entregó; necesitaba que él escuchara la verdad primero, sin filtros de cinismo.

"Mi padre, Elias, estaba siendo rastreado. No por la policía, sino por otra persona", reveló, detallando la brújula, el microchip y el testimonio del cerrajero. Luego señaló la foto de su camioneta. "La policía no la vio. Buscaban alcohol y velocidad. No detectaron el rasguño secundario en el retrovisor del pasajero. Creo que alguien estaba obligando a Elias a salir de la carretera, empujándolo directamente a tu camino para que pareciera una muerte clara por conducir ebrio."

Ethan finalmente dejó caer el cuchillo. Cayó silenciosamente entre las agujas de pino. Miró los informes, luego a Stormy, su incredulidad transformándose poco a poco en una comprensión ardiente. "La conducción errática… la Hidrocodona", murmuró, su mente reprocesando rápidamente sus propios recuerdos de aquella noche. "Recuerdo un parpadeo. Una luz repentina detrás del sedán, no solo faros. Pensé que eran las copas jugando una mala pasada. Pero... si había alguien más involucrado..."

La inmensa y paralizante culpa que había llevado durante cinco años—la vergüenza de ser un *asesino*—se estaba deshaciendo, reemplazada por el amargo y clarificador shock de ser un peón.

La miró, con los ojos ahora encendidos, no de rabia hacia ella, sino de una furia feroz y dirigida hacia el enemigo invisible. "Maté a un hombre, Stormy. Seguía borracho. Eso es culpa mía. Pero. No lo maté. No provoqué el choque." "Exacto", confirmó, sintiendo un alivio al ver que él no rechazaba las pruebas, solo la idea de su relación. "Te usaron. La persona que siguió a Elias sabía que estabas en ese camino, sabía que estabas borracho y sabía que tu error sería la tapadera perfecta para un asesinato."

El ambiente entre ellos cambió al instante. El muro de alienación moral se derrumbó, reemplazado por un enemigo común y un objetivo compartido y vital. El conflicto ya no era *nosotros contra la memoria de mi padre*; *éramos nosotros contra el verdadero asesino*.

Ethan se levantó. No intentó alcanzarla, sino el bloque de cedro y su cuchillo, pero esta vez guardó el cuchillo con seguridad. "¿Quién estaba siguiendo a tu padre? ¿Por qué?" "No lo sé", admitió Stormy. "Elias solo era el encargado de una librería. Pero era meticuloso. Era reservado con la chip. Ocultaba algo, Ethan. ¡Algo por lo que valía la pena matar!" Por fin miró el anillo de compromiso en su dedo, y esta vez, la mirada no mostraba amargura. "Has venido hasta aquí. Te has puesto en riesgo. Por fin me has dicho la verdad." "Te he dicho la verdad porque te quiero", afirmó simplemente. "Y me niego a dejar que el verdadero asesino gane dos veces llevándose a mi padre y destruyendo al único hombre honesto que he conocido." Ethan se acercó, limpiándose el serrín de las manos. Sus miradas se cruzaron y, en ese momento, la relación romántica quedó en segundo plano. Lo que importaba era el vínculo de confianza absoluta y aterradora.

"No reconstruimos sobre el amor, Stormy", dijo, las palabras resonando en su última conversación. "Reconstruimos sobre la justicia. Limpiamos mi nombre y llevamos al verdadero asesino ante la justicia." Él extendió la mano y apretó suavemente la suya, apoyando el pulgar en el anillo de madera. "Me acabas de devolver mi segunda oportunidad. No mi vida, sino mi verdad. Dime por dónde empezamos."

Forty-Nine

Capítulo 10

Juntando todo

Stormy y Ethan regresaron de las montañas sin detenerse, impulsados por el café y una urgencia ardiente. Ya no eran amantes en negación, sino parejas unidas al peligro y a la búsqueda de la justicia. Fueron directamente a la librería de antigüedades. El señor Peterson, atónito pero profundamente aliviado al ver a Ethan, les dejó entrar de buen grado en la tienda cerrada.

"Elias no solo gestionaba la tienda", afirmó Stormy, barriendo con la mirada la madera oscura y el cristal. "Escondía algo aquí, algo por lo que valía la pena matar. El chip de la brújula prueba que fue rastreado. Se desvió para sacudir el rastreador, y el asesino le obligó a subir al camión de Ethan para cubrir sus huellas."

"La respuesta no está en las piezas nuevas", dedujo Ethan, con la mente aguda, sus habilidades de carpintería aportando una nueva perspectiva. "Está en las antiguas. Elias hizo mucho trabajo de restauración. Si ocultaba algo, lo integraba en la madera. ¿Dónde guardaba sus herramientas justo antes de...?"

Peterson señaló una pared de muebles antiguos sin etiqueta que Elias había estado restaurando personalmente para un cliente de larga duración. "Estaba obsesionado con esa vitrina. Pasaba todo el tiempo en la carpintería. Decía que necesitaba hacerla 'invisible'."

Ethan fue directamente a la alta vitrina de caoba. No usó palanca; pasó las manos por las esquinas, buscando discrepancias en la veta de la madera que solo un artesano conocería. Sus dedos se detuvieron en una costura aparentemente sin costuras cerca de la base.

"Usó un porro de mariposa aquí", murmuró Ethan, con la voz tensa. "El vínculo más fuerte, pensado para ser permanente. Pero él diseñó una liberación de línea de cabello."

Trabajando con dos ganzúas metálicas finas, Ethan pasó por alto la articulación. Un panel se deslizó y reveló un compartimento oculto forrado de terciopelo. Dentro no había una joya ni una tarjeta de memoria, sino un pequeño diario encuadernado en cuero y gastado.

Stormy arrebató el diario, pasando las páginas. No eran los pensamientos diarios de Elias; era un registro meticuloso. Fechas, horas, lugares y códigos. Reconoció un nombre al instante: Harrison.

El diario revelaba que Elias no solo había estado siguiendo la colección de *antigüedades*; había estado registrando los movimientos de un receptador de alto nivel que usaba la tienda como tapadera para blanquear. Elias se había dado cuenta de que ese receptador manipulaba programas específicos de libertad condicional/rehabilitación para reclutar reclusos recién liberados para su operación—internos cuya desesperación los hacía vulnerables.

Un nombre se marcaba repetidamente: Sr. Harrison.

"Harrison", susurró Stormy, el nombre de su supervisor VSO—el hombre que firmó su programa fabricado, el hombre que llamó a la liberación de Ethan un "milagro". "No solo firmó tu liberación, Ethan", se dio cuenta Stormy, con el rostro pálido. "Te atacó a ti. Vio tu remordimiento, tus habilidades de carpintería y tu aislamiento. Manipuló tu expediente VSO para conseguirte una liberación rápida, te metió en el edificio de apartamentos que controlaba y usó al señor Peterson como tapadera para un trabajo. Te estaba preparando para que te unieras a su organización."

El rostro de Ethan se endureció con una fría claridad. El remordimiento inicial que sentía por estar borracho quedó completamente eclipsado por la malicia deliberada de su verdadero enemigo. "El programa VSO era una herramienta de reclutamiento. No estaba rastreando a Elias; estaba rastreando el *microchip*. Elias debió copiar la logística de la operación, quizás de los archivos VSO, en un chip."

"Elias descubrió que Harrison estaba usando su tienda y la ciudad afligida de su hija para dirigir una empresa criminal", concluyó Stormy. "Cogió el chip, lo puso en su llavero para ocultarlo, y Harrison se dio cuenta de que Elias era la filtración. El choque fue Harrison neutralizando la amenaza y eliminando al testigo, usando al hombre que intentaba reclutar como la tapadera perfecta y desechable."

El diario tenía una última entrada: hora y lugar de reunión, garabateados apresuradamente en el margen: *martes, 22:00. Anexo Riverbend, patio principal.* Fecha fijada para mañana por la noche. "Es un intercambio de seguridad", dijo Ethan, tocando la entrada. "Harrison debió de pensar. Elias iba a revelar el chip o usar la información. Debe ir allí regularmente." Stormy miró a Ethan, el amor feroz y el propósito compartido superando todo el dolor pasado. "Te incriminó una vez, Ethan. No tendrá una segunda oportunidad. Vamos a

Riverbend mañana por la noche. Le damos lo único que quiere—este diario—y obtenemos la verdad." "Usamos la misma mentira que él construyó", estuvo de acuerdo Ethan, posando su mano firmemente sobre la de ella. "Lo atraemos a la luz."

Fifty

Capítulo 11

El ajuste de cuentas de Riverbend

El Anexo Correccional de Riverbend era más tranquilo por la noche, envuelto en sombras que suavizaban el alambre de púas y el duro bloque de hormigón gris. La reunión estaba fijada para las 22:00 en el aparcamiento del personal, un lugar de vigilancia constante pero con tráfico limitado fuera de horario.

Stormy y Ethan estaban aparcados al otro lado de la calle, observando. Habían hecho una llamada, no a la policía todavía, sino al señor Peterson, que esperaba en una cafetería cercana, listo para marcar el 911 en un semáforo preacordado. Necesitaban la confesión completa de Harrison en el registro, no solo la evidencia circunstancial del chip y el diario.

"No confiará en mí", susurró Stormy, agarrando el volante con las manos. "Sabe que me he expuesto. Esperará una trampa." "No tiene elección", respondió Ethan, con voz baja y constante. Llevaba la misma ropa prestada que el día de su liberación, una declaración silenciosa de su honesta redención.

"El diario de Elias es demasiado valioso. Compromete toda su operación. Harrison necesita eliminar el diario y a las dos personas que lo han leído."

Stormy le había enviado un mensaje a Harrison hace una hora: *tengo la información que Elias Thompson tenía en la mano. Encuéntrame en el aparcamiento del Anexo Riverbend, a solas. Quiero una explicación antes de hacerlo público.*

Exactamente a las 10 de la noche, un sedán negro elegante y sin distintivos entró en el aparcamiento. El señor Harrison apareció, impecablemente profesional con un traje oscuro, el rostro sereno pero los ojos agudos y calculadores. Sostenía un pequeño estuche negro.

Stormy salió del coche sola, llevando el diario de cuero abiertamente. Ethan permaneció oculto, listo para intervenir si la conversación se volvía peligrosa—y sabían que así sería.

"Stormy. Esperaba que nuestra relación pudiera haber terminado sin este drama", dijo Harrison, con un tono de decepción paternal, no de pánico.

"Terminó cuando coordinaste una colisión fatal y incriminaste al único hombre inocente al que se suponía que debías rehabilitar", replicó Stormy, caminando hacia él y deteniéndose cerca de una pesada barrera de hormigón. "Usaste la muerte de mi padre para reclutar activos para tu red de blanqueo. Usaste al VSO como canal. Por eso Ethan salió tan rápido."

Harrison suspiró, con una expresión teatral de fatiga. "Reclutamiento es una palabra fea. Prefiero *la integración de activos.* Ethan era un candidato perfecto. Inteligente, excelente ética de trabajo, cero contactos externos y paralizado por la culpa. Habría sido obediente e imposible de rastrear. Tú, Stormy, fuiste una complicación inesperada." Abrió su maleta, revelando fajos de billetes. "Dame el diario. Puedo hacer que la pérdida de tu familia sea un poco menos dolorosa. Digamos, ¿medio millón? Puedes llevarte a tu prometido y empezar esa vida en las Rocosas."

"Mataste a mi padre, señor Harrison. Atacaste a Elias después de que copiara tus códigos de red en un microchip. Luego usaste la camioneta de Ethan como bala", acusó Stormy, apretando el diario con más fuerza. "Eso es asesinato." La fachada de Harrison finalmente se resquebrajó. Su rostro se torció de rabia. "¡Elias estaba interfiriendo! ¡ Descubrió que estaba usando su tienda de antigüedades para mover capital! Y tú—patética y afligida—¿pensaste que podrías salvar mi mejor recurso? No pudiste salvar a nadie, Stormy. Solo complicaste una operación limpia."

Dio un paso amenazante hacia él. "¿Crees que no os vi a los dos? ¿Esa pequeña historia de amor en mi sala de ingreso? Fue patético. Usé a ese idiota de Mark para desenmascaros porque sabía que la vergüenza haría que Ethan huyera. Casi funcionó. "Habría funcionado", la voz de Ethan cortó la oscuridad. Salió de detrás del coche, entrando en la tenue luz de la lámpara del techo, su presencia sólida e implacable. "Si ella no hubiera encontrado el chip."

Harrison se quedó paralizado, sus ojos saltando entre ellos. Se dio cuenta de que el diario era el menor de sus problemas. Tenían el motivo y el testigo.

"Vance. Deberías haberte quedado en las montañas", gruñó Harrison, metiendo la mano en su chaqueta.

Ethan se lanzó hacia delante, agarrando la muñeca de Harrison antes de que pudiera sacar un arma. El enfrentamiento fue brutal y rápido. Ethan, impulsado por años de culpa reprimida y la furia justa de ser incriminado, fue aterradoramente eficiente. Estampó a Harrison contra la barrera de hormigón, inmovilizándole el brazo. La pequeña pistola de alto calibre que Harrison intentaba alcanzar cayó al suelo. "Cumplí cinco años por tu encubrimiento", gruñó Ethan, con la cara a pocos centímetros de la de Harrison.

"Ahora sirves por asesinato." Como si fuera una señal, un repentino coro de sirenas sonó a lo lejos. Stormy ya había pulsado el botón del pequeño dispositivo que Peterson le había dado—un simple localizador. Peterson se había movido de la cafetería al borde del solar, grabando todo el intercambio.

En cuestión de minutos, el aparcamiento estaba lleno de policías. Harrison fue esposado, gritando sobre corrupción e interferencias, pero su confesión capturada por la grabación discreta de Peterson era innegable.

A la mañana siguiente, Stormy y Ethan estaban sentados en su pequeño y vacío apartamento, con la luz del sol entrando. El apartamento estaba listo para ser entregado, pero no estaban rotos. Ethan tomó la mano de Stormy, frotando la madera suave y cálida de su anillo de compromiso. La verdad no los había destrozado; los había recocido. "Todavía tengo que responder por mi crimen, Stormy", dijo Ethan en voz baja. "Conduje borracho. Quité una vida. La condena por asesinato se levanta, pero el homicidio involuntario sigue siendo."

"Y lo servirás con integridad",respondió Stormy, apoyando la cabeza en su hombro. "Pero no lo servirás solo. Limpiamos tu nombre, Ethan. Eres un buen hombre que cometió un terrible error y fue usado por el mal. Esa es la verdad sobre la que construimos."

"¿Y tú?" preguntó, mirándola desde arriba. "¿Las mentiras?" Stormy sonrió, una sonrisa genuina y pacífica, libre de la sombra de Elias y la oficina del VSO. "Me mantuve en la luz, Ethan. Confesé, busqué la verdad y arriesgué todo por ti. Mi penitencia ha terminado. También me gané mi redención. Llevó su mano a sus labios, besando el anillo de madera. "Entonces solo queda una cosa por hacer."

Tres meses después, Stormy y Ethan estaban en una montaña con vistas al valle cerca del campamento forestal. Ethan, ahora legalmente exonerado de los cargos de asesinato, cumplía el resto de su condena por homicidio involuntario mediante servicio comunitario y formación profesional en la remota instalación, un camino que abrazó con renovada humildad.

Se casaban la semana que viene, una ceremonia tranquila a la que asistían solo el señor Peterson y algunos amigos de confianza. Ethan metió la mano en el bolsillo y sacó un objeto pequeño y pesado. Era el llavero de brújula plateado de Elias, meticulosamente reparado.

"El cerrajero arregló el traqueteo", murmuró Ethan, dándole la vuelta. "Pero Elias solía decir que eso le mantenía 'yendo hacia el norte puro'. Creo que significa seguir tu brújula moral interna, por difícil que sea el camino."

Se lo entregó a Stormy. Ella presionó la brújula contra su corazón. Ambos se habían alejado de la luz, pero al buscar la dolorosa verdad, habían encontrado el camino de vuelta a un camino de honestidad.

Su amor ya no era un secreto construido sobre el dolor, sino un viaje compartido forjado en peligro y cimentado por la verdad. Su segunda oportunidad se ganó, no se les concedió.

Fin

www.ingramcontent.com/pod-product-compliance
Lightning Source LLC
LaVergne TN
LVHW020626100826
845148LV00012B/2072

* 9 7 9 8 2 3 4 0 6 0 5 8 7 *